WILD SILK

ZARA DEVEREUX

piatkus

PIATKUS

First published in Great Britain in 1997 by X Libris
This paperback edition published in 2012 by Piatkus

A CIP catalogue record for this book
is available from the British Library.

ISBN 978-0-349-40045-7

Typeset in Sabon by M Rules
Printed and bound in Great Britain by
Clays Ltd, St Ives plc

Papers used by Piatkus are from well-managed forests
and other responsible sources.

MIX
Paper from
responsible sources
FSC® C104740
www.fsc.org

Piatkus
An imprint of
Little, Brown Book Group
100 Victoria Embankment
London EC4Y 0DY

An Hachette UK Company
www.hachette.co.uk

www.piatkus.co.uk

Chapter One

The surgery was about to close when Merran walked under the shell-shaped arch and through the glass-panelled front door. The reception area had a friendly atmosphere, with its Edwardian surround and graceful circular staircase. There was nothing clinical about it. It could have been a private house.

This is one of the bonuses for being in a small country town, she decided, saying to the motherly body behind the desk, 'I've an appointment with Dr Medway.'

'He's waiting for you, Miss Faulkner. Room four,' the woman answered, with a smile that could only be called roguish. There was no doubt in Merran's mind that this respectable female had the hots for Dr Medway. 'You're his last patient for tonight. I see you're down for another inoculation. Going somewhere nice?'

'South America,' Merran said and, though used to exotic locations, she could still hardly believe it. She liked to say the words aloud, just to convince herself it was true.

'Lovely,' the receptionist responded politely. 'On holiday?'

One of the disadvantages of small-town life was the nosiness of the population, though Merran preferred to think they were genuinely interested. She had certainly given them food for gossip over the years, as had her parents before her.

'Yes,' she replied, and headed for Oliver Medway's consulting room. It was easier not to go into details. She so often flitted off abroad that folk were accustomed to her extended holidays.

No carefree jaunt this time, she thought as she stood outside the doctor's door. I'm on a mission.

Her skin tingled, little shocks of excitement raising the fair down on her limbs. Her destination was Brazil and the very name had an evocative ring. She remembered her grandfather quoting a poem by Rudyard Kipling, with lines that went: 'Something hidden. Go and find it.

Go and look behind the Ranges – Something lost behind the Ranges. Lost and waiting for you. Go!'

How much she missed him, that genial, bluff military man who had been father and mother to her after her parents' premature deaths. Brigadier David Carter, explorer, historian and eccentric. It was five years now since he had had a fatal stroke and, in an attempt to bury her grief, she had plunged into a hedonistic lifestyle, appearing to be wilder and more abandoned ever than any of her jetsetting friends. She had earned the reputation of being a cold-hearted man-eater.

'But you've done it, Brig,' she addressed him mentally as the surgery gradually quietened, wintry darkness beyond the tall windows of the corridor. 'You worked a flanker with that codicil to your will. I'm ready to inherit, but you want me to go adventuring first. All very Indiana Jones. On your head be it.'

She tapped on the door, and a deep, cultured voice called to enter. The softly lit room was a familiar one, rather shabby, with an old-fashioned treatment couch, the only concession to modernity being the state-of-the-art PC sitting on the flat surface of a heavily carved desk. Yet she knew Oliver to be as scientifically tuned-in as any graduate fresh from medical school.

He rose to greet her, a bulky, ruggedly handsome man with close-cropped, silver-sprinkled hair and alert crystal blue eyes. A casual, well-cut charcoal-grey suit draped his broad-shouldered body, the trousers loose yet somehow underscoring the generous sexual equipment of a mature man.

Merran felt her nipples crimp and heat rush between her legs. She had always had a thing about Dr Medway, right from the time she was a teenager. As the family doctor, he had attended her and the Brigadier, a solid, dependable part of her life when all else was chaotic.

'Merran.' Oliver held out a hand and she slipped one of hers into that warm, smooth paw, thrilling at the touch.

'Hello there,' she said, returning his smile and settling herself in a chair on the opposite side of his desk. As she crossed her black-stockinged legs she was aware that the silky gusset of her panties was damp, her female juices conjured by the mere presence of this man.

'No after-effects of the jab?' he asked, one of his bushy eyebrows lifting quizzically.

'No. Are there really so many nasty diseases in Brazil?'

His smile deepened, and he picked up a pen, tipping it slowly end to end as he considered her thoughtfully. 'There are where you're proposing to go,' he said. 'That was an odd thing for the Brigadier to do, wasn't it? Sending you off to the jungle. Have you any idea what it's like?'

'I've seen *Mosquito Coast*,' she replied. 'And watched wild-life documentaries.' Then she shrugged her narrow shoulders under her black sweater and added, 'But no – I don't suppose I really know what it's going to be like. Do you?'

He shifted in his chair, muscular legs stretched out under the desk and aimed in her direction. 'Well, no – never been up the Amazon myself, but I've spoken to colleagues who have. It's always been a fever spot. Unless you're a Forest Indian, of course. A great deal of it has been tamed now. Tour operators offer trips by steamer to some of the more accessible areas, but I gather that you'll be going off the beaten track.'

She nodded dreamily, listening to the cadences of his voice, which seemed to vibrate tantalisingly through her clitoris. She was sharply aware they were now quite alone in the building. From outside she could hear the footfalls of passersby and the occasional purr of a car, but these were fading.

Tawstock, a Cotswold market town, fell quiet once the shops shut, especially after dark. The only nightlife took place in the pubs, and then mostly at weekends. Merran and her GP were enclosed in peaceful intimacy, and this caused a thrill to run down her spine and connect with the deep, secret core of her.

The room was warm and she was grateful, ever a martyr to the cold. February in England was such a contrast to Bermuda, where she had been living since last summer. After touching down at Heathrow she had gone shopping in London and added to her winter wardrobe, so different from the casual beachwear of the past months.

The Polo Ralph Lauren outfit she now wore consisted of a black wool pencil skirt that clung to her slim hips and touched her ankles, a beige tweed jacket and waistcoat, and a matching beret pulled over her mane of tawny blond hair. It had cost a king's ransom, but Merran had never needed to worry about money. She didn't even glance at price tags, merely purchasing whatever took her fancy.

'The Brig explored the Amazonian Basin when he was a young man,' she said, her voice low and mellifluous. 'I think he'd rather hoped for a son to carry on where he left off, but he only had one child, my mother, and then there was me. When I came home to celebrate my twenty-fourth, fully prepared to take over Tawstock Grange, Henry Foster told me about the will.'

'Your lawyer?' Oliver asked interestedly

'And grandfather's executor. OK, so I would have inherited anyway, but once he had shown me the log the Brig had kept and the torn half of an old map, I wanted to go. I was always fascinated when my grandfather used to tell me about his adventures. They were my favourite bedtime stories.'

'You've got guts, Merran,' Oliver observed, and there was a bright, almost predatory keenness in his eyes that stabbed into her. 'I wouldn't mind tagging along, but I've too many other commitments.'

He was a widower and had brought up his two children with the aid of a devoted housekeeper. Considered to be the most eligible man in the district, he had stubbornly remained single. He sang tenor in the church choir, belonged to the music society, the sailing club and the bonsai association.

Merran was possessed of the sudden, rabid desire to crawl under the desk, open his fly, take his cock out of his pants and give him the best blowjob he had ever had. This could be the last opportunity. There was a possibility that she might never return from the trip.

It seemed that Oliver was thinking this, too. By mutual accord they stood up, and she could see the bough of his erection straining against the fabric of his trousers. Her amber eyes travelled from this promising package to his face. His mouth had softened, the lips slightly parted, and she imagined them closing over her own. Her breath shortened and her heart started to race.

'We'd better get on with that jab,' he said, without making any move to do so.

'Yes, Doctor,' she answered, and started to take off her jacket. Then, driven by a mounting lust, she added, 'Shall I undress behind the screen?'

His hands came out, gripping her slender upper arms but holding her away from him. His face was tense. 'Undress? That hasn't been necessary before,' he said, and his voice was full of questions to which she had only one answer.

'But I'm going away very soon. I shan't see you again for ages.'

'It's not bothered you in the past.'

For the first time she realised he might have resented this, and the shock of such a revelation froze her momentarily. 'I never thought you cared,' she gasped.

'Cared? My dear Merran, I've always had my vocation to consider. Doctors shouldn't get involved with their patients. It's unethical and dangerous. But I'm not made of stone and you'd tempt a saint into sin. Don't go behind the screen. Undress here, where I can see you. I'll lock the door.'

'Will you do something for me?' she whispered, hesitating by the couch, the fire in her loins mounting beyond control.

'Anything within reason,' he replied, and his hands were trembling. He pulled her into his arms and his mouth began to plunder hers, his thick, fleshy tongue delving deep, tasting her teeth, her gums, tangling with her own.

She surrendered herself to pleasure, lying limply against him, her arms lax at her sides. He was so big, so powerful a man, and she could feel the heat of his arousal pressing against her belly.

When she managed to draw breath, she gasped, 'Put on your white coat and stethoscope. That's how I always think of you.' Her eyes shone and her coral lips glistened where his tongue had moistened them.

Blood rushing with delirious anticipation, she yanked off her beret and waistcoat and pulled her sweater over her head. Her full breasts were cupped in underwired lacy baskets, the nipples hard as cherries peeping over the low-cut edge. She stepped out of her skirt and stood with her pelvis pushed forward, wantonly displaying the glory of her body. She was brown all over, wearing an expensive, year-round tan acquired in the Bahamas, Miami, California or wherever her restless feet had taken her.

A garter belt of the same cream lace and satin as the bra held up thick black stockings. Minute bikini briefs barely covered the feathery brown hair of her mons, and medium-heeled court shoes encased her slim feet with their elegant ankles, arched insteps and straight toes.

She ached for him. He was white-coated now and serious of expression, her doctor of fantasy and reality. She could see the high ridge of his phallus and longed to close her palm round it, at the same time fondling the balls in their velvety purse beneath.

'On the couch, if you please, Miss Faulkner,' he said, adopting his most professional manner. Bedside? she wondered, and a giggle caught in her throat.

'Yes, Doctor,' she replied meekly, and obeyed.

The surface was covered by crisp white sheeting, cold to her bare skin as she lay down, her head supported by a pristine pillow. Oliver stood close to her, so close that had he unbuttoned his trousers she could have taken his cock in her mouth. She turned her head towards him, lips parted and as wet as her lower, secret ones. Every sensible thought had abandoned her, leaving her melting and lubricious. The crotch of her panties had worked up into the aisle between her labia, adding its own friction.

'I'm going to give you a full examination,' he went on calmly, though his voice was husky. 'It's necessary for me to find out if your sex organs are perfectly healthy. When you get to the tropics there may be no opportunity for medical advice should these start troubling you.'

'I've never had any trouble down there, apart from an itch that needs to be scratched,' she murmured. 'I'm not a virgin, you know.'

His face, tanned from sailing, flushed to a deeper hue. 'Nevertheless, Miss Faulkner, I should be failing in my duty if I didn't inspect you thoroughly. I'll begin with your breasts.'

He reached under her, hands lingering on her firm buttocks, and she raised her torso so he could move upwards and unfasten the catch of her brassière, sliding her arms out of the fragile creation. She heard his sharp intake of breath as he stared down at her breasts.

'They're beautiful,' he exclaimed, and squeezed them gently, while his thumbs rotated on the puckered nipples.

Merran gritted her teeth and moaned, her eyes slitted as she gazed up at his intense face. She knew her breasts were perfect, had been told so by lovers, and had caressed them herself as an adjunct to masturbation, but it was exciting to hear it from the lips of this man.

He was tender in his touch, bending his head to nuzzle at her nipples, his tongue lapping at the rock-hard tips. They seemed to swell, as if trying to fill the cavity of his mouth. Merran could feel love-juice trickling from her vulva, smearing the insides of her thighs. She parted her legs almost involuntarily and lifted her pubis, the wings of her labia swollen, her clitoris hungry for pleasure.

She felt him leave her for an instant, and heard him unzipping. Turning her head towards him she saw him take his penis from his trousers. It jutted from a nest of hair, a thick, skyward-pointing weapon, the shaft veined, the bulbous, fiery head standing free of the foreskin, a pearly tear weeping from its single eye.

Her face was close, and he nudged it against her cheek, the glistening pre-emission leaving a stripe on her skin. She opened her lips and tongued the glans, dipping into the slit. He tasted salty and strong.

Adopting a sucking action, she drew his phallus into her hot, willing mouth. It felt wonderful, silky smooth, its width stretching her, its length butting the back of her throat.

She raised her hand, held his cock at the base and rubbed it gently as her lips continued their magic. Her other hand dived into the gap of his boxer shorts, finding his balls, which were all she had imagined, and more – weighty fruit ripe with luscious semen.

Oliver stood motionless, accepting the sensations she was lavishing on him. Then he stiffened, reached down and wound his fingers in her tousled hair, holding her still.

'Not yet,' he cautioned. 'Any more of your delicious mouth and I shall come, but first I must complete my examination. Raise your knees and open your thighs.'

She kicked off her shoes and splayed her legs, the air chilly on the flesh bared above the tops of her stockings. Oliver moved round till he was at the foot of the couch. He seized her hips and slid her towards him till he was between her legs.

He stared down almost reverently, as if he stood before an altar. Merran watched him in rapt concentration – those carefully manicured hands, the white linen coat, the gleaming metal stethoscope, symbols of his calling that had given her wet dreams for as long as she could remember.

She waited breathlessly for his touch, her love-bud enlarging, her vagina hungry for a cock to clutch. She kept her knees raised, gripping his hands, guiding him. He removed her panties with care, not revealing her secret in a crude way but as if performing a ritual, paying homage to her womanhood.

He brought the scrap of material to his lips, kissing it and breathing in the female essences clinging there. She remained still under his glance as it raked over her long slim thighs, flat belly, the fairness of her bush, and the darkly enticing cleft within.

Leaning closer, he parted her labia with his fingers, exposing the shining pink avenue between, then slid a finger into her, worked it around, withdrew it and trailed moisture between the pouting lips and over the needful clitoris.

'There's nothing wrong with that,' he announced, massaging it firmly. 'A perfect specimen. You should be proud of such a beautiful organ, Miss Faulkner.'

'You really think so?' Pleasure-pain speared her belly at his words and her clitoris thrummed. This was so heady a compliment that she almost climaxed.

'I do, and I think I can demonstrate it,' he muttered, his penis leaping as it protruded from his fly, still wet from her saliva and his own clear lubrication.

His fingers stroked and petted her bud, easing the tiny hood back, rubbing each side of it, tracing its stalk to where it joined her pubic bone, causing tumultuous sensations. She raised her hands and played with her nipples, pinching them into peaks, the ache within them communicating with her clit till it seemed she had three points of power.

Oliver worked skilfully, using his knowledge of the human response system. He never allowed his touch to become repetitive or boring, instead varying it, sometimes a hard friction, at others a feather-light caress. Merran could feel the waves rising from her lower back to her groin, one after the other, each higher than the last as he stimulated her gem-hard clitoris.

She was hot, so hot. The sweat broke out on her forehead, plastering her hair to her brow. Her mouth was dry, her sex wet. Her breath came in short, harsh gasps. The feeling was building, higher and higher. Rainbow shards of colour flashed behind her closed eyelids as she came in a sudden, violent welter of pleasure that shocked from her toes to her brain. She was overwhelmed in wave after wave of white-hot sensation, her body jerking, her vagina convulsing.

Her head thrashed from side to side and blindly she reached for Oliver. He reared over and positioned his cock against the entrance to her vagina. She bore down on it, feeling it impale her, filling her to the limit, chafing the spasming walls and giving her a glorious feeling of repletion.

He had waited so long for his own satisfaction that he could not hold back, plunging and ploughing, burying his shaft inside her, his balls jouncing against her perineum. Merran strained him to her, arms wound round him, legs resting on his shoulders, opening herself completely, a flower in full bloom. His hips pumped faster and faster, his prick sliding in and out as he raced towards orgasm.

Merran saw his head fall back, the thick tendons of his throat standing out like cords, then felt that sudden extra hardening and the twitch of his penis as he poured out his libation.

Later, dressed again, she sat on his knee in the leather swivel chair behind his desk. One arm was wound round his neck and her head rested on his shoulder. He smelled so good, a pungent combination of antiseptic, aftershave and semen. He held her gently, and kept raising his fingers to his nostrils, inhaling the spicy, shell-washed odour of her pudendum that lingered there.

She was indulging herself, pampering the lost little girl who inhabited her wounded heart. Oliver represented the father-figure that had been snatched from her, not once, but twice – the first Timothy Faulkner who had sired her, and then the Brigadier.

She did not like to think about her parents, imprisoning the memory in a remote corner of her mind. Better to laugh, to fling herself into the half-world of the rich and famous, to try to escape reality She shivered suddenly, as if a breeze had rippled over her body.

Oliver's arms tightened, his eyes concerned. 'Are you cold, Merran?'

She snuggled closer, pressing into his lap, feeling his phallus swelling again. 'No, just thinking. I guess I'm worried about the trip.'

He smiled and set her from him. 'Speaking of which, it's time we did what you came here for.'

She grinned up at him impishly. 'Don't worry, Doc. We've already done it.'

*

'Adrian's in the library. So's his uncle. You're late,' said Lyn bossily. 'What have you been doing? Bonking the doctor?'

'How did you guess?' Merran quipped, strolling into her bedroom at Tawstock Grange.

She smiled at her secretary-cum-personal maid, the irrepressible, bisexual Lyn Macdonald – skinny as a boy, clad in a purple leather mini-skirt and metal studded top, her claret hair gelled into spikes, her dangling silver earrings shaped like dragons.

'Are you telling me you actually got into his underpants? Not our drop-dead gorgeous medic!' Lyn sat on the ostentatious bed, original Art Nouveau and so valuable that no broker would insure it. 'Tell all. Is he well hung? Has he a monumental cock or a tiny little apology for a willie? Big-built men can be disappointing.'

'Oh, Lyn!' Merran sank down on the stool before the dressing-table that matched the bed. She nursed her sore arm and added, 'I don't know why I put up with you.'

'Sure you do.' Lyn sashayed across and perched on the edge of the dressing-table, swinging one seemingly endless, leather-booted leg. She squinted at herself in the mirror, and touched a fingertip to the mauve powder-shadow above her right eye. 'I'm your chief cook-and-bottle-washer. I organise the packing, book flights, and keep the paparazzi at bay.'

'You're good at that,' Merran conceded. 'Their interest is the price I have to pay for being born to notorious parents who came to a sticky end. And if that wasn't enough, I'm the granddaughter of a well-known, immensely rich man.'

'Aw – poor old you!' Lyn mocked affectionately, head to one side, her large hazel eyes emphasised by mascara and black liner. 'Such a drag being a millionairess and getting your photo in every upmarket mag.'

'Shut up!' Merran retorted, then, catching a glimpse of her reflection, she moaned, 'My God, I look wrecked.'

'Is it the injection or the doc? You're not falling for him, are you?' Lyn stood behind her, lifted long thin hands with purple lacquered nails and started to massage her employer's neck and scalp under the thick curtain of curls.

Merran leaned against her, aware of those tiny breasts and slight hips, needing the bliss of a quiet, loving encounter, a tingle budding in the secret garden between her thighs. Though nothing like as promiscuous as people thought, her amatory experiments had included the delights offered by female lovers, but it had not yet happened between herself and Lyn.

Till now their relationship had been informal though businesslike, but tonight Merran was acutely aware of the girl's vitality and attraction. Maybe it was time to lift the restraint imposed by their status as boss and employee.

She moved away from her a little, saying, 'You know I never fall in love.'

'It's because of your mother, isn't it?' Lyn said, and helped her ease off her jacket and sweater, taking special care not to touch the painful arm.

Then she ran her hands down Merran's spine, past the little hollow at the base and disappearing into the dark furrow that divided the rounded bottom cheeks. Merran pressed down on those clever fingers, half hoping one of them would dip into the tight mouth of her anus.

'So my shrink says,' she replied. 'She was a victim of the Charm Syndrome. Her number one was interested in nothing but fast cars and his own ego. The Brig recognised the type but she wouldn't listen, so my father drained her, emotionally, spiritually and financially. She had a career as an actress, but he drove her to pill-popping and alcohol. He was killed at a Monte Carlo rally and she took an overdose.'

'Don't let it get to you,' Lyn advised, bending her head

and trailing her lips across the sensitive zone where Merran's neck joined her shoulders. 'Not all men are total dorks. I'll run you a bath. Adrian and Mr Foster can wait. I've fixed them up with drinks and warned Mrs Harper dinner will be a tad late.'

'Liam will be along too,' Merran reminded, an instant image of him springing to mind, incredibly sexy in sweatshirt and skin-tight jodhpurs.

Liam Brent, her horse-trainer, he of the gypsy blood, fiery temper and swarthy looks, his large phallus like a serpent coiled between his thighs. Many a time she had roused that beast into spitting fury. Desire inched along her nerves as she recalled steamy episodes in the stables with him. It was not simply as a stalwart member of her backup team that she had invited him along to Brazil.

She mused on him as she relaxed in the large porcelain tub standing on clawed feet in the centre of her marble bathroom. It was filled with almond-scented water rendered smooth as satin by costly oils. The bathroom led from the bedroom, and was equally ornate and decadent in decor, keeping to the *fin de siècle*, late Victorian theme.

Lyn leaned across, working the large sponge, filling it then squeezing it over Merran's arms and shoulders. She was stripped to the waist, and the pert brown tips of her nipples stood out proud, infinitely enticing. Merran could not help touching them.

Lyn gasped and froze. Both women knew they had reached a point of no return. There was a sudden shift, a recognition. Their relationship would never be the same again. Their eyes met and their lips smiled. There was no need for words.

Merran's body glistened with a thousand jewels of water trickling over her breasts and caressing her skin, wavelets weaving amongst her pubic hair. And Lyn's fingers disappeared below the surface to part Merran's thighs, penetrate the pink folds and stimulate the ardent kernel.

Merran had enjoyed Oliver, achieved an ambition, but the silken skin, small-boned body and knowledgeable fingers of her aide promised unadulterated joy She lay back in the water, her head supported by the rim of the bath, and allowed herself to float. Lyn, gaining confidence, took off the rest of her clothes and slipped into the water. Then she lowered her head and ran her pointed tongue across the corner of Merran's mouth, advancing slowly, her movements ones of languorous grace and subtlety.

Men were Merran's preferred sex. She enjoyed their power and force and the sensation of being of little consequence in the face of such virility. But tonight she was feeling fragile, prey to unwelcome ghosts from her childhood, needing the tenderness and total understanding that only a woman could give.

They lay together in the deliciously warm water, smooth skin to smooth skin, legs entwined, hands caressing, lips testing. Lyn continued her subtle exploration of Merran's labia, softly stroking the enlarged clitoris that reared from its cowl under such delicate coaxing.

She knew so well how to proceed, and Merran became very still, letting her take charge. Passion flowered within her, spreading through every nerve and particle, and she allowed herself to be drawn into orgasm, welcoming the rush of ecstasy, falling from the heights to be held in Lyn's arms.

Adrian Foster had taken up a spread-legged stance on the rug before the roaring logs set between iron firedogs in the massive stone hearth. Crimson light flickered over the library, touching panelling dark with age, booklined shelves, rich tapestries and comfortable leather-upholstered chairs.

He swirled the amber liquid in his glass and lifted it to his lips, Adam's apple bobbing as he took a deep swallow of the vintage malt whisky. He melded into his surroundings superbly. Tall, fair-haired, charming and handsome, and his hand-tailored dinner jacket fitted his broad shoulders magnificently, crisp white poplin shirt showing off his Florida tan.

He was conversing with his uncle Henry, thick-set and distinguished-looking, the Carter family lawyer, but hardly registered what was being said. He was on edge, chain-smoking and uncertain, waiting impatiently for Merran to arrive, his grey eyes a little bleak as he thought of her.

All the way down from London she had occupied his mind, and he had wondered if he would have her that night, his penis hardening as he relived other occasions. While the headlamps flashed and the motorway unwound before him, it had seemed that the darkness was scented with blossoms and her own magical emanations.

He had imagined her hands rubbing his cock, driving him to the brink; her lips feeding on him, milking him of his fluids; her sleek limbs, her luscious sex, her wildness and passion that verged, somehow, on the edge of tears and tragedy. Her cruelty, too – her refusal to commit herself, or to love him.

He wanted to marry her, and it had nothing to do with her fortune. Unable to wait, Adrian had paused at a service station, parked the BMW in a shadowy area, switched off the engine, opened his fly and massaged his hard-on till he came into his monogrammed handkerchief. Only then had he been able to continue his journey.

Now, when at last Merran entered the room, his cock rose again. He was sure she was even more lovely than the last time he had seen her. She wore a peacock blue satin sheath. Its low neckline emphasised the curve of her breasts, and her nipples lifted the fabric in two widely spaced points.

He longed to fasten his lips round them, to suck and bite them through the material. His penis throbbed and moved against his silk underpants as he stared at the deeper shadow formed by the apex of her thighs and wondered if she was wearing panties, searching in vain for a betraying line. She often went naked beneath her expensive gowns. He could almost smell the combination of *Joy* and her own sweet nectar. He abandoned his pose in front of the fire, fearful that his erection would be noticeable.

She advanced, smiling, fully aware of and amused by his lack of control over his wayward prick. 'Adrian. How goes it? Nearly ready to leave? I hope you've bought snakeboots and a bushjacket, had your jabs and fixed yourself up with a gun.'

'Don't worry, darling. I'm fully equipped, as any intrepid explorer should be.' He grinned at her and her body responded. What woman in the drifting, partner-changing circle in which they both moved did not grow wet and desirous when he strode across her field of vision?

She knew his uncle had tried to interest him in business, but though Adrian had gone through the motions of attending university he had no need to worry about a career. His mother had left him well off, and with his good looks, breeding and confidence, he was an extremely sought-after stud.

There was a disturbance at the door, and, 'Sorry I'm late,' exclaimed Liam, bursting in. He was followed by Lyn, flamboyant in a green plastic skirt no bigger than a lampshade, a scarlet satin bustier and gold lurex stockings.

'That's all right,' Merran assured him, watching Adrian bristle. There was no love lost between these two attractive men, and she suspected that, apart from the usual clash of male egos, it had something to do with herself.

Smiling impudently, Liam came across and lifted her hand to his lips, hovering over but not touching her skin. The warmth of his breath was enough to make her clitoris swell within its moist folds.

He straightened and looked into her eyes, his own peat-dark and shining, matching the hair that curled below his collar. Not much taller than her, he was wiry and strong, putting his own unconventional stamp on the midnight blue velvet evening jacket, brocade waistcoat and black trousers so tight that they might have been sprayed on, his manhood very much in evidence.

'Ready for the trip, Brent?' Adrian drawled, staring down his patrician nose at this interloper.

'You bet,' Liam answered laconically, no way disturbed by Adrian's hostility 'It'll be successful. Ma read the cards for me yesterday, and saw it all – a river so wide you can't see the banks, and huge mountains. There'll be danger, of course, but we'll pull through.'

'Superstitious bullshit,' Adrian snapped hastily, adding aside to Merran, 'Why the hell did you ask him along? He's nothing but a jumped-up stable-boy.'

She stepped closer and her breasts grazed his chest. Looking up into his angry eyes, she ran her fingers over the satin lapels of his dinner jacket, then dipped lower. His cock stiffened beneath the expensive cloth of his trousers as her hand passed over his crotch, firm enough to be felt and fast enough not to be seen.

She said sweetly but with an underlying edge, 'This is my show, Adrian. No one else's. I'll include who I like.'

'Bitch,' Adrian muttered, in torment. 'Can I come to your room later?'

'I'll think about it,' she replied, and moved away.

'And how do you really feel about the trip, Merran?' asked Henry Foster, offering her his arm as they moved into the dining room in answer to the gong.

'It's a challenge. I needed something like it to stretch me.'

She glanced round the room with satisfaction. It was hers now – all hers. She was already accustomed to acting the hostess. There was nothing to it really, the hard work done by her housekeeper, Mrs Harvey, and Griffen, the butler.

It was they who had cared for the manor under Henry's guidance while she was away. Thus it had been kept in trust for her, that gracious old house which had been in the family for over three hundred years. Merran loved every stick and stone of it, her home – her heritage.

One day, she promised herself, one day when I've finished roaming, I'll settle down and raise children here, little replicas of those portraits of my ancestors that line the walls. And who shall I select as the sperm donor? That remains to be seen.

'I've talked over the phone to Miguel Garcia, and he's looking forward to seeing you. Once you've shown him your bit of the map he can begin planning the expedition,' Henry informed her quietly as they took their places at the oval table shimmering with antique silver, china and glass. He lowered his voice still more and added, 'Of course, as I've already said, it's vital to keep quiet about the treasure.'

'Don't worry' she whispered conspiratorially. 'I trust Adrian, Liam and Lyn, but I've only given them the barest details. The only other person who knows is Dr Medway and doctors are like priests, aren't they?'

Henry nodded his grizzled head. 'I guess so. Don Garcia is very concerned that you be careful. Brazil can be a trouble spot. Plenty of people there who'd like to get their hands on the map.'

'What's he like? D'you know him?' she asked, as a footman served the main course, the air redolent of roast lamb, boned and stuffed with mushrooms, crisply browned potatoes and vegetables tossed lightly in butter.

Henry paused, fork halfway to his mouth. 'No, I don't, but his father, Don Roberto, had been the Brig's comrade during a former expedition. Miguel has inherited the Garcia fortune, and his father's private papers. You can't get anywhere without his cooperation.'

'It'll be a crack. I can't wait,' Adrian put in, toasting Merran over the rim of his wine-glass.

For what? For us to be alone together in some primitive spot? He'd like that, having me to himself. Dream on, baby, she thought. Much as I like you, there are other fish in the sea.

Liam was seated opposite her. Driven as much by an imp of perversity as by the lechery he always inspired in her, she stretched out a leg under the table, lifted her foot in its high-heeled sandal and nudged it gently between his wide-spread thighs.

She felt him start, but he controlled himself, though she noticed that he had stopped eating, simply pushing the food around on his plate. His warmth penetrated her toes and she wriggled them under the heavy bulge in his trousers, the serpent awake and moving against the barrier of his trousers.

'We're ready, Mr Foster,' Lyn was saying, leaning close to the lawyer so that he could not avoid looking down her cleavage. 'One final shop and that's that. Am I right, boss?'

Merran, her toes still tantalising Liam's imprisoned cock, lifted a spoon filled with chocolate mousse to her mouth and nodded at her aide. 'You are. I can hardly contain my impatience.'

'Neither can I,' Liam remarked meaningfully, his voice making a dark current flow through her veins.

'I wonder what Garcia is like,' Merran said, and her tongue came out to lick a trace of dessert from her lips.

'Let's hope he's to die for,' Lyn offered, and raised her brimming wine-glass. 'Here's to Brazil. Has anyone warned them we're coming? Do they know what's about to hit 'em?'

Chapter Two

'Hi, there,' whispered Liam, poking his head round the door.

'You can't come in. This is the ladies' room,' Merran protested, but his voice excited her and the vibration of the engines beneath her feet communicated with her loins.

He stepped inside the small, luxurious, pink-tiled and carpeted apartment reserved for the use of female passengers.

It was deep night over the Atlantic. Everyone else in the first-class accommodation slept. Only Merran and Liam inhabited that nocturnal world. She shivered, nerves taut as bowstrings, worried about what lay ahead, yet tingling with anticipation, too. Liam shared her feelings, it seemed, or maybe he only shared the sexual tension which was so much a part of it.

He grinned and caught her by the shoulders, pushing her up against the washbasin. 'God, you're the sexiest boss I've ever had,' he murmured in his low, harsh voice. 'Feel this.' He placed her hand on the thick penis hidden inside his 501s. 'Had a hard-on for ages. Couldn't wait for the others to nod off. Adrian's got his eye on me. Doesn't like me much, does he?'

'He's OK. Jealous, that's all. Let me go, Liam. Someone might come in,' she gasped, but she could feel his hot dick pulsing with eagerness to penetrate her. She could not resist it.

'At this time of night? I don't think so, and if they do, they can just walk out again.' He leaned forward and ran his lips over her mouth, slowly and lasciviously, then slipped a hand under her skirt, coasted up her thigh and lifted aside her panties.

She gasped as he gently caressed the brown-gold floss and dipped a finger inside her. 'You're wet,' he whispered. 'Have you been playing with yourself?'

'Oh, Liam,' she sighed, her pelvis jerking helplessly towards him as he stroked the length of her labia and paused just below the tangle of hair, stimulating the tiny peak of her clitoris.

She fumbled for his buttons and thrust her hand into his fly, lifted out the solid column of flesh and started to fondle it. Liam groaned against her lips, his tongue linking with hers in a darting dance of passion.

He moved his finger faster, the exquisite sensation rising, rising till her orgasm swept over her in waves of shuddering, glorious pleasure.

He felt her come. Muttered, 'That's right. Go for it,' then lifted her.

She wound her legs around his waist and her arms about his neck. The clubbed head of his penis entered between the swollen wet lips of her sex and thrust home. Merran cried out, her vaginal walls clenching round that solid, powerful object. She moved with him, rejoicing in this primitive form of mating, feeling the hard, hairy ridge of his pubis butting against hers. His legs were trembling, his body shaking as he gave a final convulsive heave and spent himself.

She lowered her legs and stood on the floor, but kept her arms round his neck. His eyes were closed, his face relaxed as he rested his head on her shoulder. Her heart warmed towards him. Rough diamond he might be, but his loyalty was unquestioned. In that moment of clarity when her body's urges were stilled and her mind took charge, she knew she was going to need allies in the weeks ahead.

'It's gorgeous, Mark darling! Isn't he clever, Miguel? Don't you just adore it? No one at the *Baile da Cidade* will be as beautiful as me,' enthused the Comtesse Angelita Suffres.

'It's a triumph,' agreed the olive-skinned, aristocratic man lying on the deeply cushioned divan beside her, nodding approvingly towards her couturier who had just delivered his latest creation.

In actual fact, Miguel de Garcia was more interested in the dressmaker himself, so tall, willowy and graceful, a blond, blue-eyed Englishman who had survived the cut and thrust of London's ragtrade and become the most successful designer of the year. His last collection had been the talk of Paris. Everyone who was anyone wanted an outfit with a Mark Elvin label.

Even as Miguel caressed Angelita's ample breast, weighing it in his hand, rubbing a thumb-pad over the prominent red-brown nipple, so he was imagining Mark's lean and delicious rump presented to him naked.

His cock twitched and he turned to bury his teeth in Angelita's neck, wanting to hurt her and, at the same time, communicate his strength and ruthlessness to the young man.

'Oops, does it have that effect on you?' Mark cooed, fussily spreading out the rustling black-gold tissue of the triple layered skirt he had prepared for the comtesse. 'Of course, that's its purpose – to arouse the most uncontrollable erotic desires. She'll wear nothing under it, you see, and the skirt can be hitched up to display her derrière or her fanny, whichever she chooses.'

Miguel propped himself on one elbow. He was a forceful man, used to being obeyed, darkly handsome and dominating. His forebears had made their fortune in the rubber boom in the early 1900s, using the peons as little more than slaves. Before the crash came they had cannily invested in beef, buying up thousands of rolling acres of Argentinian sierra. With this background, he fell naturally into his position as master, in the bedroom or out of it.

'I think it might look even better on you, Mark,' he said pointedly, while Angelita purred as she rolled over and gripped his thigh between hers, grinding her pubis up and down it, seeking vital pressure on her clitoris.

Mark gave him a steady stare and flicked back his high-lighted quiff. 'My dear, wait till you see what I've made for myself. It's quite outrageous, and heads will turn.'

The comtesse and Miguel – who, among her innu-merable lovers, had the most influence over her – had summoned Mark to her bedroom to deliver the gown. It was the most sumptuous place in the whole of Casa Valentine, a villa renowned for its gorgeous decor.

Light and spacious with a view over the terrace, its furniture was walnut and the walls covered in cream silk with a leafy design in silver. Mirrors hung between them, reflecting the scene over and over, concentrated on the king-sized divan draped in chiffon and spread with white, handworked lace.

Curtains hung from ceiling to floor each side of the balcony windows, billowing slightly in the scented breeze. The floor was tiled, with bright splashes of woven Peruvian rugs, but the most startling objects of all were a collection of statuettes placed artfully on plinths where they would catch the eye.

Lifelike miniatures in marble or soapstone or glass, they depicted human beings in the throes of copulation. Beautiful figures lay in postures of abandonment, shapely limbs and perfect breasts displayed, hair flowing like water, their every orifice filled, either by stiff penises or the fingers and tongues of lovers.

They were captured in timeless lust, some grouped in threes or fours, forming a continual link, genitals to genitals, pricks penetrating rectums, lips fastened round breasts or cocks, each executed by master craftsmen – erotic works beyond price.

Angelita flew miles, employed agents to bid at auctions she could not attend and spent thousands of dollars in the acquisition of yet another piece. It had become something of an obsession, and she had specialists scouring the world for even older examples of erotic art.

Now Miguel was deliberately stimulating her in order to excite Mark. He had made a lifetime study of pleasure, believing that the senses should be gratified to the full, but there was a darker side, too – as those who came under his spell soon discovered.

Angelita was his more than willing accomplice. If it could be said that she loved any man, then it was Miguel. He was her mentor, her stern master, her bringer of intense sexual satisfaction.

She wriggled down, agile as a cat, sliding across his belly, rubbing her big breasts against the reddish head of his prick, pressing it into the deep valley of her cleavage, then taking it into her mouth. Relishing the subtle taste, she enfolded him in her curtain of black hair, a witch-woman brooding over her magic wand. She sucked it, worked her tongue round the circumcised knob, then slowly, inch by inch, let it sink between her teeth, across her palate till its length nudged her throat.

Mark unzipped his jeans, his eyes never leaving Miguel's body. His tongue wetted his lips as he lifted out his long, curving, pale-skinned cock. He caressed it in smooth strokes and it leaped within his fist, slippery with pre-come.

Miguel returned his stare, even while Angelita sucked him strongly. He pushed his hands in her hair and lifted her away. Disappointment blanked her face, but he smiled and kissed her, tasting himself on her lips. She clawed at him, writhing as though being whipped.

'Hush, child. Be still,' he whispered. 'I want to see you pleasuring yourself. Do it for me, will you?'

She lay immediately on her back, one hand pulling at her nipples, the other walking across the golden-brown skin of her stomach. Her fingers caressed the smoothness of her depilated mound and dipped between the pouting lips. She left her taut nipples and spread her legs, raising her pubis high, the feeling urgent.

Holding back the leaves of her sex with her left hand, she stretched the hood away from her plump bud, wetted it with her own nectar and massaged it in a leisurely fashion. Miguel's eyes narrowed as he observed her closely. He paused, bent his head to inhale the sharp, piquant smell of female arousal and allowed a string of saliva to fall from his lips, adding to her wetness.

Angelita smiled vaguely, almost at the point of orgasm. Mark was on all fours within her sight. His jeans were pulled down, the bareness of his buttocks uncompromisingly fair compared to the lightly tanned skin everywhere else. Miguel picked up a riding crop from the bedside table and strode over to him. The sunlight glistened on the silvery latex covering Mark's distended penis that thrust belligerently from the thick patch of hair covering his lower belly.

'Say it!' Miguel commanded, his accent more marked.

'Fuck me,' begged Mark, massaging his prick frantically.

'You've forgotten something.'

The swish of leather meeting naked flesh excited Angelita, her own bottom stinging with remembered pain. Her climax was approaching. She moaned, bit her lip, rubbed herself steadily, then managed to hold off, letting the feeling die back in order to prolong it.

'Fuck me, Master!' Mark yelled, a red welt scoring his skin, his phallus jerking wildly in his fist.

Again the whip descended and again, one blow following hard on the other. Mark started to come in long, creamy spurts. Miguel dropped the crop and reached over to catch some of Mark's tribute. He smeared it up the amber-coloured furrow dividing the younger man's rump, working his fingers into the tight aperture before inserting the tip of his prick, easing it in slowly

Mark cried out in pleasure and anguish combined, as Miguel sank the whole of his weapon into him. His arms clasped Mark closely and, as his pumping movements became more rapid, Angelita allowed her finger to resume its slide over her clitoris till she exploded in a cataclysmic fury of pleasure that left her shaking.

Once he had spent himself, Miguel straightened. Mark, too, got to his feet, wiped himself on a tissue and zipped up. All three were possessed of a peaceful, aftermath lethargy, but Miguel glanced at the Seiko banding his darkly furred wrist and began to dress.

'You're going to meet the plane?' Angelita asked

sleepily, shrugging the sheet up over her shoulders and snuggling into the pillows.

'No. I've sent Slater to do that. I intend to set a precedent. She can wait for me.' Miguel, as suave and controlled as if he had just attended a board meeting, stood before the mirror and smoothed a comb through his blue-black hair. He eyed Mark in the glass and added, 'Can I give you lift?'

'No, thanks. My Porsche is outside.' Mark gave both of them a radiant smile, then bent over and kissed Angelita's averted cheek. 'See you later, darling.'

'Ummm ... yes ... come to dinner some time. Meet our visitors ... your fellow English. Bye ...' she murmured drowsily.

It was late morning when the gleaming jet glided smoothly in to land at the International Airport, Rio de Janeiro. Merran flinched as she stepped from the cool interior and was engulfed in a great, humid wave of heat.

She was feeling disoriented. It had been a long haul. First the drive to Heathrow, then hurtling through the star-spangled night towards the spectacular dawn on the other side of the Atlantic. She had slept after making love with Liam, and had awakened to glimpse fanciful cloud formations, followed by the sight of a vast green landmass in the distance, edged by miles of bewitching coast-line.

The plane had taken a scenic skydive past the gigantic figure of the Corcovado Christ and the Sugarloaf Mountain and drifted down into the tangle of bays, capes and verdant crags contrasting with ultra-modern buildings.

'Rio,' Adrian said, taking her arm. He was amazingly spruce and uncrumpled and had even had a shave. 'Fabulous jewel of South America. It's paradise, if one is rich. If not ...?' He made a slicing gesture across his throat.

Merran knew he had been there before, whereas it had been one of the few places she had not visited. Now she viewed it with a slightly jaundiced eye, its lush tropicality almost vulgar after the wet and windy England she had left a scant thirteen hours ago. There was a nervous gnawing in the pit of her stomach at the thought of meeting Miguel Garcia, while the idea of shortly entering the rainforests caused a warm, prickly sensation between her legs.

The terminal was like any other bustling travel centre with harassed-looking passengers just arriving or about to depart, the women with hand-baggage, the men with briefcases, the children either overtired and weepy or uncontrollably active. Merran squared her shoulders, ready for the fray. Lyn was busy with Customs and luggage, as were Liam and Adrian, so she must cope alone with that major aggravation, the paparazzi.

She could not avoid them, was unable to reach the haven of the lounge before being besieged. For a terrifying instant she found herself stranded like a shipwrecked vessel amidst a sea of faces. The reporters subjected her to a rapid fire in Portuguese which she did not understand, Spanish with which she was partly familiar, and broken English.

'No comment – no comment,' she repeated, trying to push through them, her temper rising.

'Miss Faulkner, how long are you staying in Rio?' one particularly persistent young man with greasy hair and acne kept repeating, blowing his sour breath into her face. 'Is it true you are to marry Don Miguel de Garcia? What do you feel about this? Have you known him long? Is he coming to meet you? Are you staying for the carnival? Will you be attending the Civic Ball?'

Flash! Flash! Questions, always questions. She had never become used to this prying into her private life.

She took off her Ray-Bans and tried to see across the crowd, searching for Lyn.

She could not find her, but to her intense relief spotted Adrian. He scowled when he saw what was happening, his wide shoulders cleaving through the mob. They recognised him, pressing for details of his friendship with her.

He had already spent a frustrating time with Customs and now shouted, 'Get the hell out of the way, will you?'

He put an arm round Merran, shepherding her towards the swinging glass doors. The persistent little newshound followed, fresh on the scent of further scandal.

'Aren't you Adrian Foster, Miss Faulkner's most frequent escort?' he insisted.

This was too much. Merran had been grilled in London, for her name and Adrian's had been linked so often that the papers were all set to make something sensational out of their travelling together. Her head was beginning to throb, the sweat trickling down her back even in this air-conditioned reception area.

'Fuck off!' Adrian shouted angrily, glaring at the reporter.

'Leave it,' she hissed, pulling at his arm.

A camera was thrust at them, and she could almost see the compromising photo with its accompanying headline – 'Merran Faulkner, heir to the Carter fortune, in affray at Rio airport. Adrian Foster, rumoured to be her boyfriend, arrested during scuffle.'

'Having trouble?' Liam said, appearing suddenly through the mêlée. 'Are you OK, Merran?'

'Yes, yes. Let's get out of here,' she pleaded, but the reporter had other ideas, pushing his companion forward, armed with a camera.

Liam made a grab for it and was about to draw back his arm and land a punch when—

'*Vamos, amigos*, before I call the police!' a masculine voice shouted menacingly from somewhere behind them.

The reporters began to sidle away. A few further quiet, chilling words and the photographer blanched and promised to destroy the film.

Merran stared, dumbfounded, at the owner of the voice. She felt an instant pulsation in her depths, recognising instinctively that this man was dangerous. But who was he? Could it be Miguel Garcia?

He towered over the heads of everyone, long-limbed, whiplash lean and arrogant. Merran experienced a weird sensation, and it was not entirely caused by adrenalin.

It seemed as if the airport melted away leaving them alone with only a few, fragile feet between them. His eyes met hers, the hardest, greenest eyes she had ever seen. She responded by an almost imperceptible movement of her hips. Her nipples thrust against the thin cotton of her dress, twin peaks of desire aching to be caressed by those big, sinewy hands.

He was striking, if not exactly handsome. His nose had been broken at some time and he had a little scar by his right eyebrow. His hair was long, straight and brown, and that same sun which had given him an even, toasted complexion had bleached the top layer. Two firm tendons sculpted the lines of his neck down to where they met his shirt, open over the light coating of crisp hair covering his chest. He was scruffy, his chin stubbled, a pair of tatty old jeans slung low on his hips and drawing attention to the generous, priapic swell behind the faded fly-front.

The flagrant masculinity of this extraordinary vision was affecting Lyn strongly, judging by the muffled 'yummy' noises issuing from her throat. Before Merran had time to gather her wits and control her basic urges he was at her side, nodding gravely. The floor seemed to roll under her feet, but it was only the trembling of her knees.

'I guess you're Miss Faulkner, judging by the reaction

of the press,' he said. His voice was low-pitched, with the drawling intonations of Louisiana.

'I am,' she said aloud, thinking, Rhett Butler or what? He's got to be a drug-smuggler or gunrunner at the very least.

There was something in his manner that now made her hackles rise, as did the way he was regarding her lazily through a masked expression, a coiled alertness in his indolent stance.

Despite this, she was still quivering from the impact of his raw sexuality Annoying he might be, but there was no denying his attraction. She was struck by his eyes – piercing, cold as Arctic ice. They were electricifying, and there was an element in their depths which she could not fathom. Mockery? Condemnation? Desire? It was impossible to judge.

Adrian's response to him was immediate and uncom-promising. Antipathy flared. The air seemed to crackle with it. The stranger eyed him steadily, a sardonic smile lifting his lips.

'Thanks for your help,' Merran said quickly, amazed at how normal she sounded, for she was utterly thrown by this man with the searching eyes. She retreated into dignity.

'You stopped a fight,' Liam announced gleefully, smiling at the stranger as if he was a long-lost brother. 'I was about to bust that bugger's nose.'

'If you'll excuse us, we're expected in the lounge,' Merran said calmly. 'Thanks again for your help. Perhaps we'll meet sometime.'

'I was following orders,' the stranger replied, standing at ease, booted feet slightly apart, thumbs hooked in his leather belt. 'I'm Nick Slater. I've been sent by Don Miguel. He's detained, but will be here in a while. So, on his behalf, *seja bemvindo* – welcome to Brazil.'

So there was to be no getting rid of him just yet, Merran thought, saying, 'You're a friend of his?'

She slipped her hand into the crook of Adrian's arm. To prove something to this tiresome individual? To prove what? That she was already spoken for? Never had she felt more confused.

'Hardly a friend. I work for him,' Nick answered laconically, falling into stride as they went towards the lounge. A heavy, perhaps, hired to protect Miguel? He had the build. Would he be going on the trip? she wondered, and immediately visualised a kind of *Romancing the Stone* adventure.

She frowned. It must be the heat getting to her. This

man riled her. No, that was an understatement. She actively disliked him, but could not fail to notice the impression he was having on most of the other women as they entered the modern, sleekly furnished restaurant. They were positively drooling.

Lyn whispered, 'What a hunk! He certainly floats my boat.'

'Really? He doesn't do anything for me,' Merran replied frostily.

'No? Will you look at that mouth? It's sooo kissable. He's sexy as hell, a right bad-ass, and I'll bet people fall over themselves to avoid rattling his cage.'

They were shown to a table near the plate-glass windows overlooking the landing strip. Beyond glimmered the city, the sea a wide strand of heavenly blue. Merran slipped along one of the leather banquettes with Lyn following and the men sat in cane chairs opposite. A waiter appeared and hovered attentively, napkin folded over one arm.

'Try the Brazilian draught tbeer,' Nick suggested surprisingly matily to Liam and Adrian. 'We call it "chop". And the coffee's brilliant. It's called *cafezinhos*, and it's great if you have a hangover.'

The drinks arrived and Nick raised his glass to Merran. 'Here's to your stay, Miss Faulkner.'

At that moment a group of people entered. Nick rose slowly to his feet as they approached, and the lines each side of his mouth deepened as he nodded to their leader, drawling, 'Good morning, Mr Garcia.'

'Good morning, Slater,' came the clipped reply. 'That will be all for now.'

It had not seemed possible that Nick's eyes could grow any colder but this happened as he stared at his employer. Then he picked up his hat, nodded to the men and looked at Merran in a way that made her nipples rise. He smiled briefly, and stalked off without a backward glance.

'Miss Faulkner?' the newcomer purred, his fascinating accent crawling down her spine and into her core. 'They told me to expect someone exceptional, so you must be she. I'm Miguel de Garcia. I hope Slater has been looking after you. He's my foreman, a useful fellow, but tends to get above himself.'

This suave individual bowed over Merran's hand. She found herself gazing into a pair of inscrutable dark eyes. He was older than she had first thought, possibly nearing forty. Wickedly attractive, possessing an unnervingly sinister sensuality. She guessed that behind the charm lay unplumbed depths, layer upon layer – and her senses responded, yearning towards him, needing to learn everything he could teach her.

He was slim-hipped and broad-shouldered, his blue-black hair expensively styled, and he wore a loose-fitting white linen suit and Gucci shoes. Everything about him proclaimed class and wealth, in that order. Here was no parvenu, but someone with a pedigree as long as Merran's own, descended from Castilian noblemen who had joined the Conquistadors.

His thin, aquiline features were smiling, his manners formal, even a touch old-fashioned, and his clothing was faultless, bearing the hallmark of Italian craftsmen. But, in spite of this, she caught a whiff of something primitive, almost feral, beneath the camouflage of Calvin Klein's *Eternity*. He was on one side of her, Lyn on the other, with Adrian and Liam watching. The air seemed to quiver with wild pheromones, floating around her like invisible seeds.

She was suddenly beguiled by the strange pattern of destiny she saw unrolling before her. Brazil! What did it hold for her? And was the intriguing Nick Slater yet to cross swords with her?

The car was open-topped and Merran gratefully lifted her face to the breeze, her hair streaming behind her.

Miguel was at the wheel of a sleek vehicle of showy American design blazing with chrome, guiding it through wide streets banked by skyhigh buildings sparkling under the relentless glare of the sun. They were alone, the rest following in another vehicle piled with luggage.

Rio appeared to have everything – shops, theatres, business centres, long stretches of sandy beaches and lines of waving palms. Behind it lay the mountains, covered with deep green jungle. Music throbbed all around, from the honking of taxis to the strains of bossa nova pulsating from car radios.

'It's busier than usual,' Miguel explained. 'The carnival is the highlight of the year.'

'I've heard about it, of course, and always wanted to come, so my timing is right,' she replied, wondering when they were going to get down to the real reason for her being there.

'Well, yes, though this is the rainy season, which won't be so good for travelling. The rivers rise to flood levels by the end of it, around July.'

'I see,' she replied, feeling the sweat trickling down between her breasts and lodging at her waistband. Even with the breeze blowing off the sea, Rio was humid.

Miguel's opaque shades reflected her face as he glanced at her. 'Of course, I've told no one the real reason for our expedition. We don't want this known. There are villains in Brazil who'd be only too eager to get their hands on rare Inca artifacts, if such these prove to be. I hope that you, too, have been discreet.'

'Oh, yes. I was warned by my solicitor. The people who've come with me think we're simply exploring the region.'

'This leads to the Arpoador section, where the best people live,' he informed her as they left the town.

'Have you a house here?'

'No, but I've a friend who has.'

She was making conversation, all too aware of his high cheekbones like coffee-coloured cream, and feeling the light pressure of his thigh beside hers-on the bench seat – muscular thigh covered in crisp white cloth. His hands were slim and brown with tapering fingers, the nails almond-shaped. The tantalising thought occurred that he would, no doubt, know how to play on a woman's body as if it was an exquisite instrument.

She parted her legs slightly under her flimsy skirt, and the costly calf-skin seat embraced her buttocks and the valley of her sex. She was hot there, the tiny silk gusset wet with sweat and female secretions. The dampness increased as she remembered Nick Slater's mocking eyes and animal attraction. Miguel had put him in his place and she told herself she was glad. He could keep his distance, as far as she was concerned.

The road wound precariously high above the sea, which glinted in at least three shades of blue. 'Did you know that Rio-born women are famous for their looks?' Miguel said quietly, glancing at her again. 'It's said that if you take the grace of a palm-tree, the zest of a breaking wave, the sun's sparkle, the softness of a jungle flower and the fire of a tiger and stir them all together, then you have a perfect recipe for Rio girls.'

She laughed, low in her throat. 'They sound great.'

'D'you appreciate female beauty, Merran? You don't mind if I call you that, do you?'

'Of course not,' she answered instantly, but was wondering what he meant by his first question. Whenever he spoke it was as if there was something hidden beneath the surface.

'And you enjoy making love with members of your own sex?' he persisted, and his right hand came across to rest on her knee.

'That's rather a personal question, Miguel,' she chided,

but could feel his fingers moving, caressing, her skirt sliding up so that he touched bare flesh.

'Don't take offence. I think we will become good friends, you and I, on a very personal level,' he continued imperturbably, his eyes on the white road. 'You'll be spoilt for choice here. All the children of the *Cidade Maravilhosa*, the marvellous city of Rio, are stunning. Male or female, it doesn't matter. I like both. But I always think of Rio herself as feminine. She curls so invitingly round the bay. Her movements are slow, sensual, her breath heavy and warm and sweet. Like her lovely children, she tempts you, fascinates you, challenges you. Accept everything she offers, Merran, and enjoy. I do.'

This was an astonishingly frank statement from someone she had only just met, but Merran could feel herself growing warm and lubricious under the influence of his voice and the dazzling freedom of his words. They turned into a tree-lined avenue and paused at towering wrought-iron gates that bore a bronze plaque reading, 'Casa Valentine'.

It looked impregnable, as did the smooth-surfaced, high white walls topped with glittering broken glass that stretched on either side for what seemed miles. Miguel spoke into his mobile and, after a moment, the gates rolled silently open.

A private road stretched before them, and in a short while the building came into view. The roof was of red slate, the stonework pinkwashed stucco interspersed with blue and white *azuela* tiles, the whole structure set between trees and bougainvillaea bushes. The gravel drive circled a marble basin. There a fountain shot high in the air, dazzling droplets cascading over a stone satyr poking his grotesque phallus into the deep crease of a naked hermaphrodite's posterior.

Does this set the tone? Merran mused. Will the Casa Valentine prove to be Liberty Hall?

Miguel braked and came round to hand her out, then led her up some shallow steps and through the open front door into a tiled hall with arches leading off in various directions. There was a total lack of formality. No one challenged them. There were sounds of voices, laughter and the splash of water from somewhere at the back of the villa.

Merran relished the dim coolness after the grilling sunshine. She slipped her feet out of her sandals, wriggling her toes at the delicious sensation of cold Carrara marble. This changed to warmth again as they came out on a paved terrace by the side of an irregular shaped pool lined with sparkling turquoise mosaic.

A couple of swimmers pulsed through the water while the gorgeously languid or merely somnolent took their ease on benches made comfortable with flat cushions. A blanket of heat hung in the air. It shimmered with the heady perfume of sweat, sunlotion and sexual promise rising from nearly nude bodies.

On the far side was a lounger upholstered in white, where a woman basked like a magnificent cat. A young man lolled beside her, a leopard-print posing pouch barely containing the impressive bulge at the joining of his thighs.

He was lithe and well muscled, his skin browner even than the woman's, marked here and there with the scars of old wounds. His features were those of the gypsies from Andalucia, his eyes and rumpled hair jet-black. He threw Merran a sultry smile.

The woman waved, pushing back the smoky glasses that shaded her eyes. 'Miguel! Come over here at once. I can't wait to meet your visitor,' she cried, in a rich, melodious voice. 'Look who's turned up. Pépé Belmondo, my star of the bullring. He's come from Spain for the Easter corrida in Mexico.'

Merran found herself being scrutinised by the violet-blue eyes of this bizarre beauty whose raven hair was piled high on her shapely head. She was naked except for a minute white G-string that accentuated rather than hid her labia. Like the petals of a flower, they protruded either side, hairless, deep pink and alluring.

Her figure was voluptuous, and her big, firm breasts were crowned with prominent nipples. Her body glistened with oil and she possessed a deep, savage, seamless tan.

'Hello, Pépé. I saw you fight in Madrid last season. You gave us an afternoon of great emotion,' Miguel said solemnly to the young man, then added, 'Merran, meet your hostess, Comtesse Angelita.'

Merran extended her hand. Angelita sat up, slid her arms round Merran's waist and drew her down into a scented embrace. Merran could feel her whole body throbbing in response to this glamorous woman.

'You're most welcome. Any friend of Miguel's is a friend of mine,' Angelita gushed. 'Get undressed, Merran. It's too hot to do anything but sunbathe and swim.'

'And make love,' put in Pépé, his voice guttural and thickly accented, his shining black eyes expressing undisguised admiration as they fastened on Merran's breasts and long, slim thighs.

Her skin prickled. Here was a young man who faced

death every Sunday afternoon during the Season – death in the form of several tons of ferocious animal especially bred for its courage. Everything primitive in her vibrated in response, seeing in her mind's eye the arena blazing under the hot sun – the sand – the brilliant costumes – the swords – the blood.

'You should have been a boy, m'dear,' the Brig used to say to her. 'You've the brave heart of a man. You fear nothing and nobody.'

This was not strictly true, but adventure appealed to her, that need to test her endurance to the limit. Had she inherited this from her father, who died at the wheel of a racing car?

And Pépé? He, too, stared death in the eye. How would it be, she wondered, to lie with such a person – to feel the power and sense the danger? He seemed to be offering to share it with her.

'You want him?' Angelita murmured, her fingers tracing over Pépé's scars. 'Shall we have him together, three in a bed? I'll arrange it, darling.'

An affirmative hung on the air between them, enchantment breathing out from the handsome pair offering themselves to Merran, but the spell was abruptly broken by the arrival of Liam and Lyn.

'My secretary, and – I don't know how to introduce him exactly,' Merran said with a smile, 'but at home Liam trains my horses.'

'Ah, your *domador*. This is one of Nick Slater's jobs for Miguel. He, too, understands horses.' Angelita said, gracious and smiling, putting everyone at ease.

'I wanted Liam along if we're going into the wilds,' Merran explained, while he grinned at her and dropped an eyelid in a wink.

'But of course. Miguel tells me you want to see the jungle. You simply must, darling, it's spectacular. Your friends are very welcome,' the comtesse assured her, then suddenly gave a shriek of delight as she saw Adrian walking out from under the shadow of the dark. 'What a lovely surprise!'

In an instant she had flung herself into his arms, one leg coming up to encircle his hip with a flash of pussy lips divided by white thong.

'Hello, Angelita,' Adrian answered, smiling down into her face, his hands moving over her bare, glistening back and slipping down to cup the lush mounds of her bottom and toy with the deep crease that separated them.

'This is heavenly!' she enthused, kissing him. 'Where have you been hiding? I've missed you.'

'Bullshit,' he responded good-humouredly, and she led him over to her lounger.

Merran experienced a pang of annoyance. So, the oh-so-devoted Adrian had been on intimate terms with her hostess, had he? But when the comtesse looked at her and undulated her glorious body, she could do nothing but respond to the promise in those slanting, feline eyes.

'Kyle will show you to your room, darling – and yours, too, Lyn. Strip off and come back here for drinks,' Angelita ordered.

She clapped her hands and a lithe Filipino houseboy appeared. She ran her fingers over his bare chest and then let them slide lower, briefly caressing the prominence in the front of his shorts. 'Do anything the young ladies want, Kyle,' she instructed.

'Yes, madame,' he replied with a bow and a flash of even white teeth.

Merran and Lyn exchanged amused glances, and then followed him along the cloistered walkway to a pair of carved doors with porcelain fingerplates and lion-headed handles. He opened them with a flourish, standing back and saying, 'Your room, Miss Faulkner.'

'Where's mine?' asked Lyn, slanting him a glance, the

tip of her pink tongue coming out to wet her lips like a cat viewing a bowl of cream.

'Next to this one. Come this way, please.'

'I'll come any way you want, baby,' Lyn murmured, so quietly that only Merran heard.

The room was luxurious and, silently, they trailed after the young man to another door. He flung it wide. 'Your bathroom.'

The walls and floor were of blue tiles, and in the middle was a oblong sunken tub with gold dolphin taps. Merran was accustomed to splendid houses, but the villa surpassed anything she had yet seen. She was sorely tempted to have Kyle fill the tub and join her in it, but suddenly Nick's face flashed across her memory.

She recalled his behaviour in the airport lounge before Miguel arrived. He had sat staring at her through a veil of smoke curling from the cigarette in his sun-browned hand, his face hard. He hates me and all I represent, she had thought and it had been like a brand searing her mind.

The recollection made her desire shrivel and die, yet she was furious that a brief meeting with such a flinty-eyed, disagreeable man could upset her so much. To Lyn's obvious chagrin, she dismissed Kyle.

'Shall I unpack?' Lyn asked huffily.

'Do it later. There's no hurry. Why not come for a swim?'

Lyn blew out her cheeks and fanned herself with her hand. 'I'm dying for a cup of tea. D'you think they know how to make it here?'

Merran smiled, already peeling off her dress and rummaging in one of the cases for her bikini. 'Call Kyle and find out.'

'Excellent idea!' Lyn leapt for the door to her room. 'Tea and sympathy administered by a boy with skin like gold velvet. I'll do a test-run on him, shall I?'

'Go ahead,' Merran nodded.

Pépé, Miguel, Kyle – new men who all excited her. It was they who had made her feel so horny, nothing to do with Nick, she told herself firmly. Naked now, she revelled in the freedom, never happier than when in a climate where clothing could be reduced to a minimum.

She was wearing a little triangle of black satin that just covered her feathery pubic hair. It was supported at the sides by thin chains ornamented with beads. Two small pieces of material, equally bejewelled, made up the brassière, but she hardly ever wore it.

She stuffed it into her beach-bag, along with a towel, a bottle of coconut oil and her Polaroids, then stood before the full-length mirror on one wall, raising her arms above her head to pin up her hair. She drew in her ribcage, flattening her stomach, then dropped her arms, running her hands down the svelte length of her thighs which curved into dimpled knees, then out again to the gentle swell of her calves.

The languorous heat, that irresponsible sense of tomorrow-will-do which she knew to be the philosophy of tropical countries, flowed through her entire being. She lifted her breasts, held their weight in her palms and pinched the nipples between thumb and forefinger. Her body was laved in heat, the rushing, urgent heat of lust. She needed no one but herself to satisfy it, yet allowed her mind to dwell on men. How would Miguel make love? She suspected he could be a little cruel and her spine arched, pushing her breasts higher.

Angelita had promised they might share Pépé, and a threesome would be a new experience. Though Merran had almost deliberately fostered a reputation for promiscuity, it was not strictly accurate, more of a blind to shield her vulnerability. Those who were permitted a glimpse beneath the surface had dubbed her cold, but this wasn't true either. One day, maybe, she might meet someone she could trust and allow that closeness she denied lovers even at the moment of climax.

Dreaming, she stood in front of the mirror, hip thrust forward, her weight on one leg, the other relaxed, her pose one of classical perfection. As if watching someone else, she saw her hand drift down across her belly and dip into the scrap of fabric. She pushed the bikini away, plunged her fingers into the denseness of the crisp hair and circled her hungry clit.

Opening her legs, she thrust up her pubis and saw the mirror image rubbing the pink slit that appeared through the plumes, the fingers silvery with moisture garnered from the mouth of her vagina. She stroked herself, used her other hand to stretch the labia open and up so that her passion-point stood out like a miniature penis. The membrane was deep pink with passion, delicate, almost transparent, the blood coursing through it, filling it, rushing it towards orgasm.

Merran moaned, frantic for fulfilment, straining to grasp the fruit dangling just out of her reach. As the sensation grew into a mighty tempest, so she saw Nick Slater – his green eyes glittering while his lips fed at the fount of her womanhood.

She convulsed as the lightning struck, even as she

watched herself coming in the mirror, seeing her finger moving, the honeydew shining – her clitoris frantic and stiff.

'Ah, she's having it! Look! How beautifully she brings herself off!' Miguel breathed, pressing his penis between the golden orbs of Angelita's buttocks.

'Yes, yes! And I'm coming too!' she whispered, her voice riven with excitement, her hand working busily on her own slippery cleft.

Both of them were staring raptly at the vision of Merran displayed by means of the trick mirror in her bedroom. They had to be quiet, for the room they occupied was next to hers, where the mirror became an observation panel.

Angelita had slipped a chiffon shirt over her thong, and Miguel still wore his suit, though the trousers were down about his knees. Even as Merran stood there, panting after her exertions, and Angelita squirmed as the final contractions of pleasure pulsated through her, so Miguel speared her. His hands grasped her hips and spread her opening wide, his penis thrusting in, seeking to pour forth its libation.

Chapter Three

Miguel was already at the poolside when Merran returned. He was stripped to a jockstrap, sunning himself on one of the benches, swarthy and perilously attractive, a sable pelt lightly coating his limbs and chest.

The sun was lower and the terrace deserted except for Angelita and her intimates. Completely naked, she lay on her stomach with her gleaming bronzed back and rump exposed. Pépé was in the water and Adrian occupied the space next to Angelita, solidly handsome in the briefest of linen shorts, a tall glass of rum and iced lime-juice to hand.

Miguel drew up a lounger for Merran close to his own. 'Would you like a drink? Might I suggest you try *batidas*?' he said, looking round for Kyle. 'Where's the boy? Never here when one wants him.'

'I'll think you'll find he's taking care of Lyn,' Merran answered coolly. 'Angelita did tell him to do anything that was required.'

Miguel smiled like some dark prophet about to reveal a simple truth. 'We could look in on them.'

'I don't imagine they want to be disturbed.'

'Who said anything about disturbing them? Do you like watching people making love without them knowing you're there?'

Merran's face flushed and the hot sensation was echoed between her thighs. 'I've never spied on anyone,' she exclaimed, yet suddenly wanted to.

'No? Is it true then, the things I've heard about you?' he asked slyly.

'And what are those?' A dozen possibilities flashed through her mind while he continued to study her with those unnerving reptilian eyes.

'That despite your reputation, you are in reality an Ice Maiden. Are you a sham, Merran, possibly virginal underneath?'

'You may think what you like. I don't wish to discuss it,' she answered grittily.

'Ah, a woman of mystery,' he murmured, and his body betrayed his interest.

'Perhaps,' she replied uneasily, averting her eyes and trying to relax, offering her oiled body to the sun.

Adrian, watchful though appearing to be indolent, interrupted their conversation. 'It's a great time to visit,' he pronounced. 'Rio's packed, everyone keen to join in.'

'I have tickets for the Carnival Ball at the yacht club,' Miguel replied, bland as milk, though his cobra eyes continued to feed on Merran.

'I should have warned you to catch up on sleep before we got here, Merran,' Adrian continued. 'It's a crazy party, when the entire city rockets off into orbit and doesn't come back to earth for four days and nights.'

'It's so exciting, and everybody gets laid,' Angelita added, her eyes dancing. 'D'you remember what happened last year, Adrian?'

He nodded, stretching out his muscular legs and clasping his hands behind his head. 'I fell in love with you – for all of twenty-four hours. It was what you *cariocas* call a Carnival Romance.'

'Indeed it was.' She rested her hands on his fly and began to rub it, lightly and rhythmically.

His penis rose against her palm, and then he clamped

his own hand over hers and removed it firmly. 'Later. There's a time and a place,' he reminded with a quirky grin.

'Oh, very well,' she said, then fished under the sunbed and produced a bottle of lotion, adding with a subtle smile, 'I need a little more oil – just between my shoulders. Will you smooth it in?'

'You never give up, do you?' he answered indulgently, and knelt beside her, poured a puddle into his cupped hand and trickled it over her skin. The air was fragrant with the aroma of coconut.

'Never, *caro*,' she murmured, limp beneath his expert hands as they lingered lovingly over her back before dipping beneath her armpits to fondle the breasts pressed against the cushions.

Pépé was there in a flash, dripping water, fierce and beautiful, his sex boldly emphasised by the wet tanga that cradled it. 'Why didn't you ask me? he demanded.

'Pépélito – baby – it's nothing. Adrian and I are old friends,' Angelita cooed. 'Just like brother and sister.'

He continued to scowl, all heavy eyelids and sulky mouth. 'You'll come with me to Mexico?' he demanded.

'I've said I'll think about it, but there are things I have to do with Miguel,' she replied and, while responding to

Adrian's caresses, she made swirls in the damp hair on Pépé's chest and teasingly tweaked his nipples.

His lips drooped petulantly as he lay on the tiles beside her, muttering, 'Miguel! Always you favour him.'

There were strange ripples in the ether. Pépé looked as if he was about to burst into tears. Brave matador he might be, but he was no match for the comtesse.

Merran decided it was not her problem. She had other matters on her mind. Apart from warning her to be circumspect, Miguel had not yet discussed the purpose of her visit. Everyone seemed to be wrapped up in the carnival and obsessed with one another's bodies. She had not come all this way just to party.

She regarded Miguel from behind the smoke-screen of her glasses and said, 'This is very pleasant, but haven't we business to talk over?'

His lips curved in a tight smile, and he replied without looking at her. 'I'm naturally curious to read your grandfather's notes, and once we've examined the completed map we can start making plans. I've already alerted Slater, though without telling him anything. He'll organise transport at Manaus. But just for now, stop worrying and enjoy yourself.'

Merran felt a stab of irritation and, rising, plunged

into the pool, the shock of cool water, the delight of its caress on her hot skin soothing her. Maybe he was right, and there was no hurry to finalise details. Her temper had steadied by the time she resumed her place, but hardly had she settled down when a man strolled on to the terrace. He was accompanied by a youth wearing holey blue jeans, a sleeveless vest, with a stud in his nose and a cropped haircut.

The older man went over to kiss Angelita warmly, then said, '*Buenos dias*, my darling. How beautiful you're looking. Having fun?'

'I am.' She smiled at him affectionately. 'Did you have a good trip, Raoul? Mark's finished your costume and it's gorgeous. Who's your friend?'

'Barney Jones. A guitarist. We met in Rome.'

'Hi, Barney,' she called out. He nodded in response and was dispatched to mix drinks.

'He's talented,' Raoul said. 'I can help him make some useful contacts.'

'You're all heart,' she teased, then added, 'Let me introduce you to Merran Faulkner, one of Miguel's business associates. They're off adventuring up the Amazon very soon and I'm thinking of going along. Merran, meet my husband, Comte Raoul Suffres.'

This was a surprise. Somehow Merran had not thought of Angelita as married. Raoul smiled down at her. 'I'm enchanted, *chérie*.'

He was small and olive-skinned, with narrow lips and peaked eyebrows. His was an attractive face with thin features and black hair receding from a fine brow. He wore designer jeans and sneakers, a chain bracelet on one wrist, a gold-strapped watch on the other.

He took a chair in the shade, saying, 'I don't know how you can lie in the sun, hour after hour. I'm melting. Most unpleasant. And how is it we haven't met before, Merran, on the Riviera or at Marbella?'

'You're there often?' She, too, was wondering the same thing, and vaguely recalled hearing mention of Comte Suffres and his glamorous wife.

'There's nowhere like France. We've a house in Paris, and a villa in Cannes. I only come to Rio when pressed by Angelita – it's her hometown, you see – and for the sake of business.'

'What is your business?' It must be something lucrative judging by their lifestyle, Merran decided.

'Coffee,' Raoul replied. 'We own one of the biggest plantations in São Paulo. When Angelita and I married, two of the greatest coffee families were united. Not that we don't love, admire and respect each other. Isn't that so, my sweet?'

He took one of Angelita's hands in his and sucked her fingers into his mouth one by one, running his tongue over them with a kind of careless enjoyment. All the while his eyes scanned Pépé, who was lying flat on his back, his leopard-skin-covered cock pointing to heaven.

Angelita flicked her husband playfully on the nose. 'That's absolutely true. I adore you. But this one is mine. You've brought your own.'

'Don't be miserly.'

'He's straight. You wouldn't stand a chance and, if anything, he'd be butch, like you.'

'Would you care to take a bet on it?'

Jet-lag was catching up on Merran and she was unable to keep her eyes open, going to sleep with their voices in her ears. When she woke much later it was to find herself alone.

A lovely hush lay over the land. The sea was only a short distance away, while on the other side the sharp jagged outline of mountains broke the skyline. It was a sight to make one hold one's breath. But though in the flesh she was in Rio, her spirit soared homewards to Tawstock Grange. She imagined she saw her grandfather and heard him say, 'Don't get sidetracked, old girl. Remember why you came to Brazil.'

Dreamily following this floating vision, still enmeshed in sleep, she unconsciously raised her hands and fondled her nipples, then caressed herself between the legs, aware of that secret delta hidden by the strip of fabric.

Suddenly she was alert. Someone was watching her. Her eyes snapped open and she yielded to the urge to cover her bare breasts with her hands.

Nick Slater was seated at one of the white-painted ironwork tables, feet propped up on a spare chair. This position pushed his fly area into greater prominence, a pronounced package straining the tight denim.

He had a cheroot clenched between his teeth, his slouch hat pulled down low on his forehead. She had no idea how long he had been there, observing her nakedness. His eyes narrowed and there was a flame in their depths. It was a look that sucked out her strength and made her womb contract. She was riven with desire, embarrassment and a tiny dart of fear.

'What are you doing here?' she shouted crossly. Swinging her legs over the side of the lounger, back turned towards him, she reached for her cotton shirt and dragged it on.

His mouth curved into a taunting smile. 'Don't tell me you're shy?'

'You've no right to be on the terrace,' she stammered. 'It's a private place for enjoying the sun without being stared at.'

He lifted his shoulders in a shrug, insolently relaxed, slumped low on his spine, the whiteness of his shirt shockingly vivid against his coppery skin. 'If you don't want to be looked at then I suggest you wear more clothes, Miss Faulkner.'

'It's nothing to do with you,' she retorted hotly, resisting the temptation to run. Her heart was thumping madly and although he had not moved, it was as if he had come suffocatingly close.

'Just as well it's not.' There was menace in his quiet tone. He raised his eyes to hers and in them she read something that almost paralysed her. 'For believe me, lady, if you were mine, no one would look at your body but me.'

'I'll report you to Don Miguel,' she said, her voice tight and controlled. She started to thrust her oil and towel into her bag, wanting to put as much distance between them as possible.

He chuckled, and his booted feet hit the ground

abruptly. Merran flinched, his every movement jolting down her spine and connecting with her loins. He tilted his hat to the back of his head, leaned forward and rested his forearms on his knees, still staring at her in that alarming, insolent way.

'Tell him what you like. Maybe it'll turn him on him hearing I was looking at your tits. He's an oddball, as you'll soon find out.'

Merran could feel a blush staining her neck and face. She clasped her shirt around her, the bag held before her like a shield. 'What Don Garcia does is no concern of yours,' she hissed.

'Time will tell,' he answered levelly. 'Now go inside and get something on. The evenings are chilly out here.'

'I'll go in when I want, and wear exactly what I like.'

He took a drag on his cheroot, keeping his disturbing eyes on her, drawing in the smoke and blowing it out through his nostrils in a leisurely way. His look seemed to whip off her bikini bottom and expose her to his gaze. Her wayward clitoris quivered. She was aware that the narrow gusset had worked its way between her labia and was now undeniably damp. Her breasts thrust upwards beneath the thin shirt, nipples hard as iron.

Nick threw aside the butt and was on his feet in one fluid motion. He came so close to her that she caught the smell of him, the strong, powerful odour of male sweat, male hair, and the musky smell that can never be banished from male sex organs, no matter how often they are washed. Involuntarily, she swayed towards him, fire licking along to the tips of her nerves.

'Jeez,' he said huskily. 'Didn't your mother ever tell you not to play with the big boys?'

'I have no mother,' she said.

She could feel herself being drawn into the blackness of his pupils and, for a mad second, longed to drown in those eyes, lost for ever. Hell would open at her feet, cunningly disguised as heaven.

His face became sombre, falling into brooding lines. He reached out a lean hand and a tingle stabbed from the base of her spine to her G-spot as one finger slowly traced over her jaw, her throat, and then her nipples, moving from one to the other with a light touch.

She shuddered, gasped, and her pelvis rose to meet his penis. She could feel it, hot and hard, through the restricting jeans. There was no sense or reason to the passion that engulfed her as his mouth closed over hers. His firm lips were dry at first, but she moistened them with her tongue, opening her mouth wide as if she would swallow him into herself.

Taste, touch, feel – the tangy savour of saliva and tobacco and a hint of rum – masculine – male – man. The word association blazed through her brain as she ground her body into his, wanting more – more – more—

He was crude, he was insolent, but now she understood the meaning of the term 'a bit of rough'. He was that, all right. No gentleman this, a scruffy, unshaven roustabout, and her nipples ached, her clitoris thrummed and her innermost haven yearned to have him enter it, pulsing, driving, possessing every particle of her – mind, body and soul.

The sky darkened with tropical abruptness. The lights came on beneath the surface of the pool, flooding it with a blue glow. Muted, opalescent spots gleamed overhead. Nick took his mouth from hers, though his hand continued its descent towards the fragile triangle protecting her mons. He started to stroke her through the thin fabric, pulling it tight so that her dewy pubic hair was visible either side of the gusset.

Someone moved in the shadow of the arch and Liam stood there, leaning his shoulder against a column. 'Time to get ready for dinner, Merran,' he said.

'Damn!' Nick swore, and his hand tightened painfully on her crotch.

'Thank you, Liam,' she said shakily. 'I'll be with you in a moment.'

'OK. I'll walk you to your room.' His concern was touching and Merran began to come down to earth. What was she doing in this man's arms? Had she gone mad?

Nick's hands dropped to his sides, but still she did not move, her naked breasts yearning towards him, her sex slick wet. 'You'd better scuttle back to your friends,' he said sarcastically. 'Go on, Miss Faulkner. Run, before you do something you may regret – like becoming a real person instead of a Barbie doll.'

She jerked away, eyes shooting sparks. 'Oh, you – you!' Grabbing up her bag, she stormed off, hurling a final barb over her shoulder. 'I can't think why Miguel has a bum like you around. I'll see you're fired!'

Nick's eyes met hers across the space between them, dangerous as spears. 'You're wasting your time. From now on you and me are going to stick close, whether you like it or not. I've not only been hired as your guide, but your bodyguard, too.'

'The hell you are! We'll see about that!' she muttered as she went inside.

Merran was thankful that her bedroom was empty, Lyn conspicuous by her absence. Recovering from the flight or screwing Kyle blind? It didn't really matter. Merran needed space in which to think.

She curled up on a damask chaise-longue by the window, staring out at the star-spangled sky. The night air was like honey. Some considerate person had ensured that a bottle of champagne stood cooling in a silver ice-bucket and, as she ruminated, she sipped the sparkling vintage from a Baccarat flute. Somewhere, in the distance, a samba band was playing.

Slowly and carefully she unravelled her thoughts. So, Nick had got to her, had he? She couldn't stop thinking about him, seeing his strong jawline, shaggy sun-bleached hair and those fierce emerald eyes. She remembered how he had finger-stroked her inner folds, and the intoxicating pressure of his tongue entering her mouth.

She squirmed against the upholstery, her bikini drawn up between her swollen love-lips. It was no use lying to herself: she had revelled in his caresses. Gloried in them. Craved more.

OK, so he was a hired man. But this wasn't the first time she had felt calloused hands on her breasts and pussy, or enjoyed ardent, almost brutal kisses and sex that was simple, direct and crude. Liam wasn't far off this, and there had been others before him, ever since she was a teenager.

But he infuriates me! she thought. No one has treated me quite like he does. It's as if he despises me because I'm rich. Needs to humiliate me and bring me down. Therefore I shan't give him the satisfaction. There's no way I'm going to fuck him, even if he was the last person alive on earth.

Restless, unsettled, filled with the urgent need for completion, she put down the glass and started to get ready for dinner. Her watch gave her seven o'clock, and she hurried over her shower, resisting the temptation to ease the ache in her clitoris. She sat on the padded stool at the dressing-table and applied *après soleil* lotion to face and body. Her skin had turned even darker during the few hours she had spent under the Brazilian sun.

She took the towel turban from her head and shook out her hair. It fell across her shoulders and halfway down her back in a thick, layered, ringletted mane.

Sometimes she grumbled to her hairdresser, complaining because she wanted a short, straight style. He was stern, wielding his scissors like rapiers as he snipped off the merest whisper of split ends while lecturing her on how lucky she was to have natural curls.

Curls she had in abundance, and curls she was stuck with, it seemed. And those same curls were repeated in the plentiful bush that veiled her pubis. She buried her fingers in it, stroked and played with it, one digit finding the hidden nub and pressing it lightly. A thrill passed through her, a hot line from her groin to her nipples.

No, she told herself sternly, and began to make up her face, using the minimum of foundation but concentrating on her eyes. Amber, catlike, they were her best feature, and she used moss-green kohl on the lids and a mascara wand to darken her long lashes.

Was it her imagination, or were her lips bruised from Nick's kisses? Maybe they were merely pouting from the passion he had evoked. She used a lip-liner, then filled in with coral. Even the feel of the brush made her squirm, reminding her of the touch of his tongue.

Angelita glided into the bedroom just as Merran was putting the finishing touches to her toilette. Her violet eyes deepened to pure amethyst and her glossy red lips parted as she exclaimed, 'Darling, you look gorgeous. Good enough to eat.'

'Thank you,' Merran answered with a smile. Her first dinner party in Rio and she had taken pains with her appearance.

'I love the gown,' Angelita continued, eyeing the sinful white creation that clung closely to Merran's curves, slit to the thigh on one side and with a plunging neck and low back. 'Surely it's a Mark Elvin? I'd recognise his stamp anywhere. He's a friend of mine.'

She was wearing a shot-silk dress that fastened on one shoulder, the colours vivid blues, bright yellow and cerise. It floated around her, giving tantalising glimpses of breasts crowned with luscious nipples, the shadowy area at the junction of her thighs and the sheen of deeply tanned flesh.

Merran gazed at her with something akin to awe, inhaling the marvellous perfume from the flower-fields of Grasse, mixed with the intoxicating oceanic exhalations from Angelita's female depths. Desire stirred within her, the need to cup those breasts in her hands and explore the hidden wonder of the comtesse's womanhood.

Angelita seemed like one of those ancient priestess-whores who guarded the temples to Isis, the Great

Mother. Her hair fell loosely about her face, and drop earrings swung against its night-dark depths. Her eyes were compelling, tilting at the outer corners to match her wing-shaped brows, the lids bronze.

'Your gems are old?' Merran said.

She rose to her feet and touched Angelita's arm which was banded by a gold bracelet six inches wide and studded with oval agates. As if of its own volition, her hand moved towards the spade-shaped pendant damascened with arabesques that rested in the valley dividing the comtesse's breasts.

'Very,' Angelita replied, her voice husky, moving her body so that Merran's fingers could not avoid brushing over the hard nipples so clearly visible through the silk. 'And I'm hoping to get even older ones, when we find the Inca treasure.'

'You know about that?'

'Naturally. Miguel tells me everything.' Angelita stroked Merran's bare shoulders with so delicate a touch it was as if she was seeing with her fingertips.

'Everything?' Merran said unsteadily.

'Well, almost.' Angelita's reply was laced with laughter.

'He's your lover?'

Angelita chuckled, allowed her hands to rest on Merran's breasts and feathered over the nipples with light fingertips. 'How quaint. He makes love to me, yes, but so do others. Miguel is my master. I submit my will to his and, by so doing, make him my slave.'

'But you seem so independent. I don't understand,' Merran murmured, her clitoris stiffening between the pouting lips of her labia.

Angelita withdrew her hands. 'You will, darling, before long. Even the strongest of us need to be controlled sometimes. Now come, it is time for dinner.'

The meal was served in a cool, high-ceilinged room with French doors opening on to a balcony. Chandeliers threw a soft glow on snowy damask, cut glass, porcelain and silverware and reflected off the heavily carved fronts of colonial Portuguese cabinets. The atmosphere was gay, larded with the excitement of party-time.

These are more my kind, Merran mused, listening to the witty, sophisticated talk that rose and fell to the accompaniment of music drifting from concealed stereo speakers.

'Villa-Lobos,' Miguel said in answer to her enquiry. 'One of Brazil's most talented musicians. This is his composition, *Bachianas brasileiras*. It is a fusion developed and perfected by a master, where the forms and ideals of Bach are melded with wholly native idioms.'

'He was never afraid to obey fresh impulses in the course of a work,' Adrian added, nodding across the table at her.

'I must get the CD,' she answered, thinking: now I am comfortable, speaking a language I understand. I don't need a caveman type who announces his approach by a series of grunts and the sound of knuckles scraping along a forest floor.

The dazzling variety of superb food was served by silent footmen wearing white. All were handsome specimens, selected by Angelita for their physique and bearing. Ugliness offended her. As each one paused at the side of her chair, offering yet another course, she reached out a hand and openly fingered his male equipment.

The dishes were traditional, hot, spicy, titillating to the taste-buds. 'It took the catalyst of African culture to turn out a national cuisine,' Angelita remarked to Merran, smiling into her eyes, knowing she had observed her toying with the footmen's private parts. 'When the slaves arrived, they brought their own knowledge of cooking. Coconut milk, dende oil, cashew nuts and the fiery malagueta pepper were added to Portuguese and Native Indian dishes, transforming them into something truly sensational.'

'Ummm—' Merran breathed appreciatively, taking a sip of wine to cool her mouth. 'I've eaten West Indian, of course, but this is unique.'

Sweeter and saltier, it was an ambigious combination, leaving one in a constant state of alertness. Traces of delicious seafood, hints of chicken and beef, all mixed with spicy rice and sauces that were out of this world. One dish after another appeared, followed by exotic desserts: ice-cream dusted with finely chopped nuts, floating in a sea of chocolate; fresh fruit piled high on silver platters, then coffee, black, sweet and strong, served in gilt-lined demitasse cups.

'It's great to be back,' Adrian remarked as a servant leaped forward flicking a lighter and holding it to the tip of his cheroot. 'I feel like some action. Who wants to go into town? The clubs will be heaving. How about it, Merran?'

She declined, but Liam and Lyn expressed a desire to explore Rio and Miguel put a chauffeur-driven car at their disposal.

'Shall we have another drink?' he suggested when he

was alone with Merran and Angelita, adding, 'Now we can talk, my dear. Don't mind the comtesse. She knows about our secret.'

Glasses were refilled and the servants dismissed. Then Merran opened her bag. 'Here's the log and half the map.'

She was feeling relaxed, though not entirely sober. Dinner had been wonderful, Angelita a charming hostess, and the conversation stimulating. She realised that now would be an opportunity to complain at Nick's behaviour, then decided against it. They had more important matters to discuss.

Miguel's eyes were lynx-keen as he took the papers from her, his fingers brushing hers, sending tiny sparks along her nerves.

'Most interesting,' he said, but his eyes were devouring her and she could not be sure which he meant, the log and map – or herself. His smile was a caress in itself as he added, 'May I borrow your grandfather's notes?'

'You may, and I'd like to see what you have.'

'Of course. I've been waiting years for this opportunity. My father told me the Brigadier would send you.' He rose and went to the elaborately decorated teak bureau, taking a little key from a gold chain round his neck and unlocking one of the drawers. He returned, carrying a manila envelope.

Inside was a matching piece of paper. Miguel moved closer, his head touching hers as they put the two parts together. Merran caught her breath. He smelled gorgeous, of the most expensive aftershave, a nutty, spicy odour with musky undertones.

With a rustle of silk Angelita came across to lean on Miguel's shoulder, examining the completed map. 'But this is amazing,' she murmured. 'Beyond Manaus, heading north into the jungle.'

'That's right. An old, forgotten route. We shall be exploring unknown territory.'

'Is it possible there are still such regions in this day and age?' Merran asked, responding to the filaments of excitement electrifying the air.

'The rainforests are huge, the mountains vast and mysterious, the rivers long, winding and treacherous. Oh yes, my dear, South America maintains her secrets,' Miguel replied, a distant look in his dark eyes as if he was seeing visions. Then he came back to reality, saying, 'Your glass is empty. Let us drink to the success of our venture.'

They drank, then freshened their glasses and moved

out to the balcony overlooking the garden. 'It's so beautiful,' Merran breathed, filled with alcoholic *savoir-faire* and losing her wariness of the comtesse and the Don.

'So are you,' he murmured, standing close to her, leaning against the stone balustrade, the subtle lighting throwing planes and shadows across his aquiline features. 'Is she not charming, Angelita?'

The comtesse was on Merran's other side. She was enclosed by these two elegant individuals, feeling their touch on her bare arms, the warmth of their bodies against hers.

'Delightful,' Angelita answered, and slid a hand down Merran's back, approaching the hollow between the curves of her buttocks.

'So lovely an English girl, fresh and sweet,' he added, and his hand slipped over Merran's shoulder and invaded the halter neck of her gown, cupping one naked breast, pinching the nipple between thumb and index finger.

She could feel her sex-lips unfurling like a bud in the sun, aware of moisture around her vulva and a pulsing in the sensitive spot at the top of her cleft. His eau-de-toilette and Angelita's French perfume seemed to be acting like a narcotic, or maybe it was the wine. Whatever the cause, she was overwhelmed by lust.

Miguel took her hand and pressed it to his groin, making her aware of the rising hardness of his penis. 'Open my fly,' he commanded.

She started, shocked by this blatant request, but obeyed him, unfastening the buttons one by one and reaching her hand into the gap. His penis leapt out and she cradled it in her palm, stroking the long, thick shaft and rubbing her fingers round the swollen, naked head. He was big – bigger than Oliver Medway, bigger than Adrian, and she glanced down wonderingly at this hard, hot weapon filling her hand.

Moisture seeped from her, wetting the narrow satin gusset of her panties and tangling with the curling bush fringing her engorged labia. She ached to feel that huge object filling her to capacity, stretching her love-tunnel, its base stimulating her clitoris.

Releasing himself, he moved behind her. She could feel the heat and bulk of him pressing into the avenue of her bottom. His hands worked on her breasts, then slid down her body and pulled up her flimsy skirt.

Angelita stood in front of her, and eased down the little strap of white silk that covered her mons. As if in a trance, Merran lifted first one leg then the other so that her panties could be removed. Her skirt was now rucked up to her waist and she was aware of the solid bar of Miguel's prick moving against her naked flesh. She lifted her hips towards it, opened her legs, willing him to enter her.

Instead, his hands came round to rest each side of her labia, gently opening her wide, her wetness glistening silver in the soft light, her clitoris enlarged and protruding as he stretched the lips apart. Angelita fell to her knees, mouth parted, the tip of her tongue coming out to lick over Merran's anguished love-bud.

It was a lively, experienced tongue, darting and flickering, playing on that sensitive nub while Merran moaned and arched her hips, pushing her pubis towards it in supplication. Miguel continued to rub his penis up and down the divide of her buttocks, the clubbed head just touching the entrance to her body, then withdrawing teasingly.

Merran rested her back against his chest and stared up at the stars, her body racked with exquisite pleasure. She forgot everything else. Needed nothing but Angelita's tongue and clever fingers pinching the pleasure-bud and holding it to her mouth, till finally Merran was carried away on orgasmic waves that made her senses reel.

At that moment, when she was panting and pulsating,

Miguel lifted her and impaled her on his cock. She cried out as the velvety walls of her vagina clenched round it, spasms of extraordinary delight shaking her entire self.

Nick stood in the shadow of a cedar tree and watched the comtesse and his boss seducing Merran. He heard her plaintive cries as she reached the extremity of passion. His heart melted and his sex hardened.

Then he strode away, got in his car, checked his firearms, and drove headlong into town.

He avoided the playgrounds of the rich, and headed for the shacks and bars that catered for the poor in the *favelas*. Like all pockets of poverty, these were breeding grounds for crime and violence, the downside of Rio which the tourist industry struggled to keep under wraps.

He braked outside a small wooden house which boasted the sign *Fonda del Commercio*. Sounds of revelry came from within, shouts and laughter and the constant beat of the salsa, the rumba – the samba.

A woman lounged on the verandah, smoking a cigarette. She was beautiful, with the exotic hothouse beauty of a mulatto. Tall, queenly, with wide shoulders, she had pronounced nipples under a tight crop-top, long thighs and taut-muscled buttocks barely covered by a leather mini-skirt.

She recognised him at once. 'Nicky,' she whispered in a husky voice, hips swaying as she moved down the rickety steps towards him.

Her hair was ebony, braided into a hundred, bead-tipped plaits. Her eyes were predatory, silver in the moonlight, and she wafted *patchouli* and the feral odour of coition.

'Hello, Carmensita,' he replied. She was a whore, but had never yet charged him.

She wriggled her hand inside his shirt, red-nailed fingers seeking his nipples, then lifted one of her long smooth legs and wrapped it round his thigh.

'Humm, he's ready,' she murmured as his cock jerked against her. 'You want me, honey?'

She was coarse and crude, selling her quim to almost anyone for a fee, but yes, Nick wanted her, needing the brief bliss of oblivion that orgasm would bring.

His hands closed round her butt, fingers aware of the texture of leather, and then he moved one hand round to the front, brushing the wiry black curls that coated her pubis. He did not attempt mouth-to-mouth contact. In common with all whores, Carmensita never kissed a client, even though he knew she did not think of him as such.

She smelled like heaven, salty and inviting, and Nick fingered her hot, wet sex and gave full rein to the lechery that stiffened his phallus and made him mad for release.

She led him to her room next door to the wine-bar, and there he lay with her on the double bed, the blankets and pillows fusty from innumerable couplings. The air was humid, her skin sweaty, his own rubbing against it, mingling his juices with hers.

He plunged his dick into her, wanting to bury himself there forever, to breathe in her strange, steamy perfume and forget the tormenting memory of tousled tawny hair, a pair of amber eyes and the sleek, clean-swept limbs of the Englishwoman, Merran Faulkner.

Chapter Four

'Wow!' Lyn exclaimed when Merran had finished dressing for the costume ball. 'Talk about Turkish Delight! Makes me feel really naff.'

This was not true, for Lyn wore an outrageously skimpy futuristic outfit, silver and black PVC that flattered her tiny breasts and lean hips, and fishnet stockings held up by gilt suspenders.

Merran had decided to go as a harem lady. Her brown legs glimmered through pale green chiffon pantaloons dotted with gold-thread flowers. A semi-transparent shift and minuscule bolero barely covered her breasts, its sides and hem fringed with seed pearl strands. She slid her feet into embroidered slippers with turned-up toes and fastened a veil over her hair, a rope of jade round her neck, matching bracelets and anklets that tinkled as she walked.

'Well, if it isn't Scheherazade,' remarked Adrian when she arrived in the salon, his eyes automatically drawn to the brownish-pink nipples pointing upwards through the flimsy shift.

He was exquisitely attired as a Regency rake in a bottle-green velvet tail-coat and high black stock. His fair hair was brushed forward in Byronic style and he carried a malacca cane and a low-crowned topper. His form-hugging buckskin breeches did nothing to conceal his cock, which had thickened at the sight of Merran.

Angelita was dressed as Cleopatra, in a decadently indecent costume. Outsized lapis-lazuli earrings gleamed against her black hair and a headdress with a jewelled serpent rested in the centre of her forehead.

Her ripe breasts, the nipples with their wide brown aureoles, were fully exposed beneath the golden collar lavishly ornamented with lotus motifs. Her white pleated skirt was slit up the front. Around her waist was a gem-studded girdle from which a panel hung between her legs. Every time it swung forward it afforded a flash of her shaven mons veneris.

They were joined by Raoul, who had taken on the persona of Pan, with hairy goat's legs, a bare torso and a pair of horns sprouting from his forehead. He trilled on a set of pipes and Barney started to dance, his short Greek kilt whirling up around his bare arse.

Merran scanned the crowded room, wondering where her bodyguard might be. She wanted to shock him with her revealing dress. Would he subject her to an unblinking stare or would his firm upper lip curl in contempt?

Miguel materialised to kiss her hand, a sleek figure in black and red. It had not taken too much effort to transform him into Mephistopheles. His eyes glowed, accentuated by pencil and shadow, giving him a truly devilish appearance.

They trooped noisily into the grounds towards the waiting cars and Angelita hung on Pépé's arm, scolding him loudly for wearing traditional Spanish costume. 'Why aren't you in your suit-of-lights? You look so sexy in it.'

'I can't put it on except for the bullfight. It's unlucky,' he muttered crossly.

'Never mind, pet. Those tight trousers are nearly as good. They show off your tush, balls and cock to perfection,' she said, testing them out, a bottom cheek fitting snugly into the palm of her hand.

The throb of high-velocity engines echoed under the trees, and the sun was poised like a crimson ball over the indigo hills, sending out great sweeping arcs of colour. A single star hung against the sky, gleaming like the diamond earring of a woman gazing dreamingly across the cosmos.

It was heart-stoppingly lovely, and Merran wanted to linger, but Angelita's imperious tones broke across her reverie. 'Come along, and don't forget your domino.'

A mask. Something to hide behind so that one could behave in any way one wanted. The masks the comtesse had provided were every bit as splendid as those worn by the Venetians long ago. Merran's was of black silk, fringed with jet, a tiny, glittering strip that covered her nose and brow, with only her eyes and mouth showing.

The ball was held at the mammoth Canecao nightclub and Miguel had booked a box. Dinner was provided but few dallied to eat, eager to gyrate to the two bands playing non-stop on a revolving stage.

Seated above the floor, Merran gazed down at the milling crowd as they swayed to the samba or smooched to the bossa nova. She was aware of the heat, the smell of sex, hormones stimulated by the proximity of the half-naked dancing bodies. It was an orgy waiting to happen – the freedom and anonymity of a masked ball.

Miguel had not been exaggerating when he had sung the praises of Rio women. Even masked, their charms were obvious – breasts ample or pert, nipples like raspberries or brown cobnuts, skin of every shade from cream to coffee to shining black. Their legs were superb, athletic or gently rounded, long, dimpled or curvaceous. Their hair flowed, was piled high or in shag cuts – sepia, red, honey blonde and platinum. Their costumes were imaginative and varied, but with one thing in common – extreme brevity, with some portion of their sexual attributes exposed.

Where they all woman?

'No, they're not,' said Raoul, standing at the rail and staring down. 'Some of the loveliest are transvestites, or have gone the whole hog and become transexuals. What a feast!'

She danced with Miguel, with Adrian, with Liam, swept into the writhing, happily sweating crowd. Everywhere people were pairing off, seeking the seclusion of the stairs, the shadows, or boldly carrying out their predilections in public. Miguel held her hard against him, prick swelling in his tights, and she remembered last night and how he had lowered her on to his enormous erection.

His hand rested on the small of her back as they danced, then went lower, pressing the seam of her harem pants into the crease of her sex, the tip of one finger working into the tight pucker of her forbidden hole.

Her nipples tingled, chafed by her thin blouse and his velvet-covered chest. She rubbed herself against him like a cat, eyes slitted in ecstasy. He nibbled her ear, then her throat, sucking and biting, arousing her unbearably. There was no let-up, no time to gain control, just the beat, the heat, and the man exciting her. She could feel his penis like an iron rod nudging her belly and could not help raising her pubis to meet it.

Miguel smiled and reached between their bodies to press his finger into her avenue and exert pressure on her bud. He probed the gossamer material concealing it, then began to stroke the pearl-shaped head, with delicate strokes that sent tremors through her body. Moist warmth spread from her vagina, wetting her pubic floss.

The crowd was thick around them, bobbing, jumping, dancing, fornicating, and no one was aware of what Miguel was doing to her, or, if they were, considered it normal behaviour for such a licentious gathering.

Even so, Merran experienced shame, but could not prevent herself from bearing down on his hand and rotating her pelvis. With no pause in the dance, Miguel continued to stroke her clitoris through the sensual gauze material. She could feel her juices soaking it as he gave her no respite; heavy, insidious waves of pleasure began to build up in her loins.

It was too late. She was going to come in front of everyone. There was no fighting it and she climaxed violently, while Miguel held her and then wiggled his silk-covered fingers inside her as he whispered, 'Yes, yes – that's right. Do it for me.'

Sinking down to earth as the orgasmic waves still roared through her, she became aware of a man looking at her.

He was dressed in sheik's robes, with an enveloping white burnous and striped headcloth. He was very tall and carried himself like a prince. He stared straight at her as her pleasure faded, and she found herself falling into Nick's green eyes. He was carrying out his duties, booted feet crossed at the ankles as he leaned against the wall, arms folded over his chest – silent – watchful.

Samba was everywhere. Down from the hills flocked the poor, gaudily bedecked in satins and tinsel which they had slaved all year to buy. Each a member of a samba school, they flung themselves into the fun, seizing the chance to taste wealth and enjoyment for a few hours during those throbbing, enchanted nights.

Rio resounded to their drums and chants, a wild cacophony of sound – bongos, whistles, and the weird yelping of the native *cuica*.

Merran found herself swept into the turmoil willy-nilly, for Angelita would not miss a moment. She led her visitors into the streets, embracing everyone she met. It was impossible to get about except on foot, for entire roads were blocked off from traffic, and samba bands played for twenty-four hours a day for anyone who wanted to dance.

Everybody did.

Adrian stayed close to Merran, having warned her not to carry money or credit cards. Pickpockets had a field day in the packed alleys, despite the strong police pres-ence. She was glad of his company, afraid of getting lost, but the people were friendly, smiling, singing, losing themselves in the miracle that was Rio Carnival. Above all, they were dancing – always dancing.

At first she hesitated, then joined in, finding there were no rules to follow. Soon she was copying the others, feet moving fast, body swaying provocatively from the hips, arms flung over her head. The music seemed to penetrate her bones, and she surrendered herself to the exhilarating sense of liberation.

Each evening there was a party at some sumptuous home or other, and then it was nearly over, one final fling and tomorrow it would be Ash Wednesday.

'Rio will awake from its bacchanalia and return to normal,' Miguel assured her. 'Then we shall concentrate on our journey to Manaus.'

The last night, and Angelita was entertaining at the villa. All day long the servants had been in a ferment of activity, though still managing to take it in turns to slip out and see the processions. Flowers filled the rooms with heady perfume, deep couches stood in readiness, buffet-tables groaned beneath a wealth of dishes, and the bar had been freshly stocked.

Merran's gown was of antique silk, so old that it had discoloured to a milky cream. It clasped her body closely to just below the knees where it flooded out into black lace, like a river foaming over a waterfall.

She had bought it in Madrid, a flamenco dress with a low oval neckline. A dress for dancing, feet stamping out a savage tempo, back arched and arms posturing towards heaven, while the fingers clicked castanets.

Her throat, upper breasts and shoulders were bare except for a lace mantilla, its cobwebbed folds rippling from the diamond-studded comb set high on the coronet of hair. She was nude beneath the dress, feeling the silk caressing her buttocks and pussy like a lover's hands. She wore black hold-up stockings and her shoes were black too, high-heeled and plain. She tucked a crimson rose behind one ear and hooked gold hoops into her lobes.

She adopted the proud carriage of a gypsy dancer and, when she reached the terrace, Angelita slipped a hand under her elbow, saying, 'How very Spanish you look. Are you wearing panties?'

A coil of desire tightened in Merran's womb. This worldly woman knew so much about female arousal. She longed to be alone with her to feel those expert fingers on her clit, and experience the enjoyment of smoothing the comtesse's bare pubis and arousing the dark red flower that bloomed between her labia.

Angelita had insisted that her party be candlelit. The band had arrived and set up their drums on the terrace. They wore multi-coloured shirts with wide frilled sleeves. Their hands beat out a driving rhythm; waiters circulated bearing salvers of canapes; the sound of popping champagne corks resembled miniature artillery.

Angelita flashed around the pool like a dark comet in her black and gold gown designed especially by Mark, tambourine thudding against her palm, its bells jingling. The crowd thinned and Merran rose from a luxurious, cushion-heaped divan, searching for a cigarette.

A pack was offered and she met Nick's sombre stare. There was the scrape of a match on a leather heel and the flicker of a small flame that seemed to draw them into unwonted intimacy.

'Thank you,' she said, the cigarette trembling between her fingers, and went to pass him.

He was as still as a panther about to spring. Though he made no attempt to touch her it was as if his fingers had penetrated her inner core. Their eyes locked and time stood still.

She wanted to walk away but those piercing eyes, deepset under brows that rose like wings, hypnotised her. Then, suddenly, Angelita called out, 'The water's divine! Come in, everyone.'

The moment vanished. Nick melted into the gloom beyond the terrace. The comtesse was already in the pool, her costly gown soaking, the bodice clinging to the puckered crests crowning her breasts. There were answering shrieks as other women jumped in, followed by men throwing aside jackets and trousers.

Angelita's immersion was the signal for an explosion of sexual activity. On couches, the tiled floor, in corners and in the open, people were copulating. Raoul mounted Barney, plunging his turgid penis into the young man's rectum while he, on hands and knees, fastened his mouth round the cock of a much older man who knelt before him.

Lyn was in her element, unable to decide which to chose and opting for both – a Junoesque *chola* girl astride her face, and a beautiful youth plunging his prick into her sex.

Wildness flooded through Merran's blood. The music beat in her head. Strong, bold rhythms born of Africa and Spain. She was aware of a stickiness around her vulva and a tiny pulse beginning to throb high up in her hidden cleft.

She had possessed few inhibitions when she arrived in Rio, but those that remained vanished as Miguel walked across to her and said, 'Undress, darling.'

He was magnificently nude, his penis rearing up from a dense forest of coarse hair. A pair of impressive globes swung in the dark-skinned scrotum beneath.

He went round behind her and unbuttoned the back of her gown. It slithered down to lie in a silken puddle around her feet. Merran stepped out of it, very conscious of her black stockinged legs and high heels. She looked like a tart, and the thought was unexpectedly thrilling, yet her cheeks took on the colour of her pink sex-lips as she realised she was exposed to the eyes of any stranger who cared to look.

Too proud to cover herself with her hands, she brazened it out, chin up, arms akimbo, legs slightly apart. Miguel nodded, satisfied. He advanced a hand and took the comb from her hair, the locks unwinding to curl over her shoulders, part hiding her breasts. He smoothed the silkiness of her stockings, then ran a finger round the elasticated lacy tops and began to roll them down.

Merran submitted as he removed the last vestige of clothing, almost, she felt, the last vestige of civilisation.

She ran to the pool's edge, dived in and came up close to Angelita who, soggy dress discarded, floated in Pépé's arms, her legs tangled with his, one hand massaging his erection. Her guests romped and splashed and played, indulging the child within and, at the same time, satisfying their adult libidos.

Merran lay on her back and gazed up at the stars, deliberately distancing herself from her body as she tried to correlate the storm of desire that had never ceased to torment her since setting foot on South American soil. Her sexual experiences prior to this now seemed almost innocent.

The comtesse and Miguel had opened her eyes and taught her body a new language – that of the darker side of passion – perverse, possibly dangerous, deliriously exciting – almost obsessive. It was as if they were challenging her to take part. And this was only the beginning.

Soon they would be thrown into even greater intimacy when they left for the jungle. Despite her attempts at rational thought, she could feel a slow, steady build-up of tension in the tissues of her sex, a surge of renewed heat invading her body.

Miguel surfaced at her side, shaking the water from his streaming hair. The pool was shallow there and he bottomed it, pulling her into his arms. He bent his head and took one of the succulent tips of her breasts into his mouth, sucking strongly.

Beneath the surface his phallus was ramrod stiff, ripe for penetration. She turned slowly to face him, placing a hand on each of his shoulders. Her legs rose up around his hips. She crossed them, pulling him closer, feeling the purplish head bumping against her opening. She guided him in.

He groaned, his fingers tormenting her nipples, lifting her high with his every thrust. Angelita swam up to them, her lips the colour of crushed pomegranates. Like a glittering golden mermaid she pressed against Merran and slid her arms round her waist. Her hands skimmed over her slippery wet belly and teased the soaking pubic hair. Then she ran the tips of her fingers round the rim of Merran's labia and touched Miguel's thick shaft as it worked in and out.

With him pumping into her strongly and Angelita's thumb fondling her swollen clit, Merran came almost instantaneously, hearing the comtesse's deep-throated chuckle caressing her ear.

It was late. They had swum, fucked, eaten of the dozen extravagant dishes and drunk magnums of champagne. Some slept where they lay, to wake later and crawl off to find another congenial partner in lechery. Some were seated, mother-naked, at the round iron tables, drinking and smoking, deep in discussion of politics or philosophy.

The samba band played on, seemingly inexhaustible.

Merran retired to her room, dizzy with champagne. She had left Miguel to Mark Elvin, intrigued to see him sinking his penis into the dress-designer's fundament. Like the band, Angelita appeared to be tireless. Pépé, Adrian and several other eligible gentlemen were acting the stud for her. Last seen, Liam had been vigorously humping a blonde million-dollar princess who owned a racing-stable.

Heigh-ho, Merran sighed, and didn't much care.

She stood on the balcony, looking out across the shimmering valley over which the moon cast a silver pathway. The lights of Rio twinkled in the bay and up the mountainside. Every now and then a toad called to its mate in triple love-notes, and the cicadas kept up their endless rasping.

The country was stunning, and every fibre of her being responded to it. Exciting, nerve-tingling, promising adventure beyond the ranges, as the Brigadier had said.

But was it only this? she wondered. Had he not, perhaps, known the other side of Rio, the darkly sensual side where every deviation could be met? Had he, too, sucked at the breasts of the gorgeous women, or indulged in a fancy for someone of his own sex?

Anything was possible, she decided, the secrets of the human heart too deep to be measured. She even had an inkling of how her mother might have felt about her father – beginning to understand the driving passions that make the most sensible women act out of character.

Wasn't she doing it herself? Wasn't she permitting her lurid imagination to create a secret heat in her honey-slick core as she wondered how it would be to have Nick shaft her?

His mouth! She couldn't forget it. A kissing mouth if ever God made one. And his fingers stroking her mound. How would it feel to have that mouth sucking her clitoris, drawing that lively little gem between his lips, licking it with his tongue?

Restlessness inched through her, but she was unwilling to return to the party. She had had enough of partying, now wanting to concentrate her energies on the task ahead. Wrapped in one of the towelling beach-robes Angelita supplied, she wandered into the bedroom, deciding that she needed a walk to clear her head.

She put on a button-fronted, sleeveless dress, and shook out her wet hair. Knickers were an afterthought, but she wriggled into a pair, then tucked her feet into toe-post sandles, took up her tooled leather shoulder-bag and let herself out of the door.

The only person she met as she looked for an exit was a swarthy waiter who grinned at her lewdly and made some remark in Portuguese which was lost on her. The drive stretched ahead, leading to the gates, and she was not sure if she wanted to go that far or even if they would open for her. She paused beneath a jacaranda tree, getting her bearings.

Her courage failed. It was lonely, with the stars like jewelled buttons in the purple sky and insects whirring faintly in the bushes. This was no way for an explorer to behave. She squared her shoulders and started to walk the length of the drive.

It was like going through a solid block of marble veined with mauve and dark green where the moonlight dripped between the leaves. She shivered, staring at the black banks of trees. Might there be snakes, sliding through the bushes or curling themselves around the boles amidst the muddle of vines? And what about the big cats, puma and jaguar? Was there one stalking her at that very moment, crawling forward on its belly, great golden eyes fixed on her, its prey?

The sudden beep of a horn shattered the silence, and

headlights stabbed through those slabs of darkness, turning them into trees again. A car drew alongside, and a low-pitched voice drawled, 'What are you doing out here, Miss Faulkner?'

Relief washed over her, coupled with annoyance because it was Nick. 'I needed a change of scene,' she said loftily.

'I'll take you where you want to go,' he answered and opened the passenger door.

'No,' she declared, chin lifting stubbornly.

'Get in!' he repeated.

'I won't!'

'Then go back to the house. You can't wander about by yourself. It isn't safe.'

'What do you care?'

'I don't. I get paid to do a job. That's all.'

'You're so damned rude.'

'Maybe. Now are you getting into this car or not? You're wasting my time.'

'You're going into town?' Changing her mind, she went round and scrambled in beside him. The leather seat was cool, striking through the thin cotton skirt, connecting with her secret lips but doing little to assuage their sudden heat.

'Can do. I've finished my rounds.' He slipped the

117

engine into gear and they rolled down to the gates, which opened automatically.

'Your rounds?' She was mystified.

'I check on the security guards.'

'Oh, I didn't realise—'

'Didn't you know the comtesse employs a small army? It's a necessity when you're a rich dude like her old man. The crime rate is sky-high in Rio. It's one of the poorest, most violent places on earth.'

'I didn't know,' she said, sitting stiffly as the car turned into the road.

'I guess you wouldn't, Miss Faulkner. Poverty won't be any of your concern.'

For the first time she noticed the gun lying on the floor near his feet. Did he always go about armed? She sneaked a sideways glance at his profile. The tip of his cigarette glowed in the darkness. In the brief glare of passing car lights, she saw his hands on the wheel, relaxed, easy, in perfect control.

He was dressed in jeans and a white T-shirt. The spasmodic blaze of flying headlamps made his skin seem almost black in contrast. He also had a faded blue denim jacket across his broad shoulders. His shaggy hair brushed the collar.

The miles slipped smoothly away beneath the speeding wheels and soon Rio swam up before them. 'Where did you want to go?' he asked.

'I'm not sure.'

There were still people about. Street-lights glared harshly on the promenades. Tired but dogged revellers waved as Merran and Nick drove by. He stabbed her a glance, remarking, 'Tomorrow Rio will be hung over and go to Mass like a repentant hooker.'

Her pulse was racing at the close proximity of his thigh, the denim rubbed white across the knees and round the fly. Her shoulder pressed against his arm on the bench seat and, when he lifted it and rested it on the back, it was as if he embraced her. He smelled fresh and clean, his hair slicked back and damp from a recent shower. A musky male scent breathed out through his pores, stirring her senses.

The heart of Rio was quiet now, except for the distant whine of police sirens. It looked as if it had been besieged by savage hordes. Sleeping bodies sprawled on pavements. Drunks sat on kerbs, holding their heads. As Nick drove through the central avenue they came upon a party of masqueraders – an Arab wandering dazedly along, an exhausted clown, a dishevelled ballerina and an African chieftain. Somewhere a die-hard samba band played on. A regiment of street-cleaners was moving in, starting to sweep up tons of debris.

'There's no doubt now that the carnival's over,' Nick said ironically.

'Where are we going?' she asked, suddenly realising that this might have been an unwise move on her part, trapped in a car with an armed man.

'To the beach.'

Merran was forced to accept that she had no one else to blame for getting herself into a situation which might prove awkward. Nick seemed disinclined to talk as they sped along the wide coast road. It was fringed by swaying palms with palatial houses and hotels on one side, miles of sand and the hissing Atlantic Ocean on the other.

'Over there is home,' she said a little wistfully.

'England?' He was certainly a man of few words.

'Yes. I don't suppose you've visited it.'

'I've been lots of places, Miss Faulkner, and England's one of them.'

This stopped her in her tracks. Somehow she could not imagine him in London, certainly not striding the streets of Tawstock. He simply wouldn't fit in. Yet she was curious. Who or what was Nick Slater, besides being one of the sexiest men she'd ever had the urge to screw?

They were nearing the furthest end of Copacabana Beach, where it joined Ipanema. Merran's blood rushed and her skin prickled as Nick suddenly slowed the car, purposefully switching off the engine. He turned to her and stared intently.

'Where are we?' she asked edgily. 'Miles from any-where by the look of it. You'd better not try anything or I'll—'

'Scream?' he interjected with a lopsided smile. 'Really, Miss Faulkner – and this from a gal who's been flaunt-ing her fanny at every goddamn man all evening.'

'I do what I like,' she stammered, nipples crimping in response to the dark-brown timbre of his voice.

'Sure you do, ma'am,' he drawled, and eased towards her. 'And to my way of reckoning, you sure like fucking.'

'Take me back to the villa.' She was tossed in a mael-strom of emotion, uppermost of which was sheer, animal lust.

'Not quite yet, Miss Faulkner. I want to show you something.'

'And what is that?'

Was he about to expose himself? She felt an instant pulsation in her belly.

'It's the beach where every New Year's Eve thousands of voodoo worshippers meet to pay homage to Iemanjá, the goddess of the sea.' He sounded serious, even intent, and the enigma of the man became even more intriguing.

'That sounds interesting,' she said after a moment. 'Tell me more. The comtessa hasn't said anything about it.'

'She wouldn't, but believe me Rio isn't all boutiques, sunbathing and screwing. Will you come?'

'I suppose I'll have to, unless I walk back to the villa.' She was cautious, edgy – excited.

She stepped out into the rich tropical darkness, filled with the almost overpowering scent of flowers and the salty smell of the sea that reminded her of her own female essences. It rumbled and foamed, crawling up the long stretch of gleaming white sand, then retreating with a low, ominous hiss. Night threw a violet mist on the water, and the moon sailed austerely overhead, accompanied by her retinue of stars.

Merran's feet touched grass, then shingle and finally soft sand still warm from the day. Although the city lights twinkled and she knew that modern apartment buildings, wide streets and mansions were not far away, she had a sense of isolation as she gazed at the vast expanse of sea and the great curve of the bay.

Little had really changed since it had first been sighted by Portuguese sailors five hundred years before. Brazil sprawled over half the continent and embraced the world's mightiest river, the Amazon. Much of it was still unexplored, and the danger, the wildness, communicated itself to her, dwarfing her problems into insignificance.

And the man strolling beside her blended perfectly into this environment where savagery lurked just under the surface.

He paused when they reached a clump of rock, settling his back against it, one leg braced on the slippery sand. The moonlight was bright as day and its pale, silvery fingers caressed his hair. Merran ached to do the same.

'It's so peaceful right now, you'll find it hard to credit how crowded it gets on New Year's Eve,' he said slowly, and she melted inside at the hard green stare of this tall, narrow-hipped man.

She rested an elbow on the giant boulder beside him and glanced down the length of the beach. 'What happens then?'

'It gets to be a place for pagan worship. The voodoo-ists come from miles around, determined to start the year right. They build little altars and lay out flowers and candles and rum, the sort of things any proud, beautiful lady might like to have – presents for Iemanjá.'

'They really believe it'll bring good luck?'

'Sure. Voodoo's powerful. The slaves brought it over from Africa. There was nothing the Catholic priests could do to stop it, though the blacks let them think they'd been converted. In reality, they kept to their old gods, just used different names to keep out of trouble. Iemanjá became the Virgin Mary, Oxalá, god of harvest, took on the name of Jesus, and the wicked demon Exú kind of turned into Satan.'

His voice rolled on as he painted so vivid a verbal picture that Merran could almost see the worshippers with their drums, their altars, the flickering candles, the dancing. The deserted beach seemed suddenly peopled with white-clad figures sacrificing chickens to their deities.

'At exactly midnight, they rush to the water's edge, carrying their offerings, and the waves get big and come slapping over the sand, sweeping those gifts away,' Nick concluded, a faint, cryptic smile forming on his lips.

Merran came to herself with a snap, glaring at him. 'Nothing magic about that. A high tide.'

'It scares you? Too raw, too primitive, too close to nature for comfort? I thought you liked to get back to basics, Miss Faulkner.'

'It doesn't frighten me and I don't believe in it,' she lied. 'I'll bet it's just another excuse for a party.'

He straightened, his face grave, and plunged a hand into his hip pocket, drawing something out and offering it to her. 'Even if you don't believe in demons, take this for protection.'

'What is it?' She was suspicious as her fingers encountered a thin chain weighted with a hard, shiny object. She held it up and saw it was a tiny gold hand closed into a fist with the thumb sticking up between the first and second finger.

'A *figa*,' he replied, his eyes glittering in the gloom. 'An amulet against the evil-eye. It symbolises fertility and passion, and wards off envy and jealousy and keeps wicked spirits in their place.'

She felt a soft, small stirring in her heart, pleased that he had given it to her. 'Thank you, Nick,' she said, conscious this was the first time she had used his given name.

He shrugged, destroying the fragile moment of communication. 'They're on sale everywhere. But to work, someone has to buy it and give it to you. It's strong magic.'

'Really?' she said sceptically, but her hand closed round it.

'Honey, when you've lived rough like I have you won't poke fun at magic.'

'Then I'll wear it. ' She gave an unsteady little laugh. 'Let me help.'

He stepped closer. She felt the intoxicating brush of his fingers against the nape of her neck as he lifted her hair, lingered, caressed her scalp, sending shock waves through her entire body. His nearness filled her with hot, carnal pleasure.

Helpless, she let him take the *figa* from her, and thrilled to his touch on her topmost vertebra as he fastened the chain round her neck. The amulet hung down between the valley of her breasts where three top buttons were undone. Nick came round in front of her, his sinewy brown fingers easing the rest from their embroidered holes till the bodice was open to the waist.

He spread it wide, exposing her bare breasts. Her taut nipples were dark cones crowning the sun-tanned orbs.

He expelled air sharply, then grazed one with the palm of his hand and toyed with it, rolling it between his fingers. Merran whimpered, and he bent his head and took it into his mouth.

Fire flamed from the sensitive tip to the fulcrum of her pleasure. As he tongued her, his thumb circled her other nipple, tripling the sensation, her clit throbbing in response.

His arms formed a cage on either side of her body, palms pressed flat against the rock. He thrust his pelvis against the curve of her belly, and she could feel the stirring of his erection and something else, too – the automatic that he wore in a holster under his jacket.

This doubled her excitement, suggestive of bravery and heroes and all the romantic fantasies that had been hers since she first became aware of the difference between men and women. Her mind fogged as she was overcome by a violent wave of desire, sex the only imperative.

Suddenly and forcefully his mouth came down on hers, tongue diving between her lips and plundering the soft wet cavern. The kiss deepened, lengthened, every recess of her mouth explored.

She could feel her labia opening, the sea-anemone

mouth of her vulva pulsing, liquid dampening the panties that barely covered her delta. Her hand went to his fly, fingers fumbling in her haste to get at his penis.

He held her firmly with the flat of one large hand, and with the other unbuckled the holster and let it drop to the sand. Then he unzipped his jeans and set his manhood free.

It was too dark to see properly, but Merran's fingers fastened round it, silky-smooth and beautifully warm, big, almost too big. Would she be able to take it all? The foreskin was rolled back from the slippery glans, the shaft thick and long. She could feel the throbbing veins, the nest from which it had sprung, the tight testicles bulging below it.

His hand swooped down under her skirt, lifting it waist-high. The ribbon ties each side of her panties tore as he tugged at them. The scrap of silk was tossed aside and lost somewhere in the dark. With one lithe, strong movement, he caught her up in his arms, then laid her down on the sand.

Merran reached for him, her legs splayed. He straddled her, jeans about his hips as he lowered himself on to her. His weight was delicious, firm but not crushing, full of controlled strength. He poised over her for a moment, his prick teasing her opening, then rolled to one side, a leg trapping her thigh. Quickly he unbuttoned her dress to the hem and folded it back. Then he proceeded to lick her, his fleshy tongue creating havoc with her breasts, stabbing into her navel, her wet mound and, finally, her clitoris.

He trailed his fingers back and forth over the swollen petals of her labia, then lapped at the tender kernel with sure strokes and subjected it to a vigorous tonguing.

She had reached that precious plateau where nothing would stop her coming and felt herself starting to ride the rollercoaster to heaven. She heard someone cry out, and did not realise it was herself, caught up in the ecstatic spasms racing through her.

Nick was there at the entrance to her sex – too big to slide in easily even though she was slick-wet. She arched up to meet him, frantic to have the hot, thick member pounding inside her. With one thrust he buried his phallus in her, its hardness shocking against her with a force that she felt in her womb and heart.

She took every inch of him, her body spasming and shaking as the feel of her tight, wet walls clutching at him sent him spiralling over the edge in a dark frenzy of release. He came into her in a series of convulsive jerks, a wrenching climax that left him shuddering.

Merran lay quite still, the fading spasms of pleasure rolling through her, his penis still buried deep. His head was heavy on her shoulder, the sweat soaking through the back of his T-shirt. She could hear his quick breathing and the pounding of his heart. To be there with him felt so natural and right – but it was far from that.

What the hell am I doing here? she thought, coming out of the trance-like daze. With *him*, of all people! I must be crazy!

She tried to move but, though he shifted his weight, his cock only slid partway out of her and lay, slightly sticky, on her thigh.

'Would you mind getting off me?' she hissed, though a portion of her wanted him to push it back in and start over.

His eyes opened and he stared at her warily. 'OK. If that's what you want.'

'I do,' she snapped, and struggled to sit up. 'Take me back to the villa at once.'

'You're the boss,' he answered, tucking his penis into his jeans and fastening up, not looking at her.

Merran stood there, prim as a nun, buttoning her dress. Her knickers were nowhere to be found. She did not intend to lose any more dignity by ferreting around for them. She resolutely picked up her bag. He towered over her, holding out his pack of Marlboro's.

She laughed without mirth. 'The post-coital cigarette? I don't think so.'

She felt as embarrassed as a teenager who has let a petting session get out of hand. Nick grinned and shook his head. 'Ouch! The lady has claws.' He reached out to caress her face, running a finger down her cheek.

'And she'll use them if you ever mention a word about this to anyone,' she shouted, jerking away from him.

'A one-off?'

'Most definitely.' She started to stalk up the beach towards the car.

'Pity,' he drawled. 'You're one hell of a lay.'

'Be quiet!'

She was throwing barriers between them in frenzied desperation. For years she had called a halt to any relationship when it started to involve more than lust. Nick might, just *might*, be the threat to her peace of mind she had so carefully avoided. The idea filled her with horror.

Lights were still blazing when they drew up at the villa, though the sun was rising in an orange halo, slitting the heavens, waking the parakeets and casting a glow on

Nick's face as he half turned, eyeing her in an unrepent-ant, taunting manner.

She jumped out of the car as if stung.

'*Buenos dias, señorita,*' he said with an impudent grin.

'Damn you!' she spluttered, fury strangling her. 'You're paid to guard my body, not fuck it!'

'Same difference,' he rejoined, jammed his foot on the accelerator and shot off into the dawn.

Chapter Five

'Goodbye, darling! Wish I could come with you, but duty calls. Be good, be careful, and don't do anything I wouldn't do. That gives you plenty of scope,' Raoul said, kissing his wife tenderly.

He stood by the villa steps, resembling a gaudy bird of paradise in his scanty silk kimono. Barney yawned, kissed her too, then leaned a lazy elbow on Raoul's shoulder.

Adrian, lounging against the bonnet of the leading car, glanced across at Merran. She was dressed for travelling in blue jeans that fitted snugly round her bottom. Her nipples lifted the fine cotton of her shirt, and she had brushed her hair back and confined it in a white scrunchie, her neck as graceful and slender as a ballerina's. Adrian's groin grew heavy, and his forehead rucked in perplexity.

He was worried about her. She had become increasingly unapproachable since Ash Wednesday, and he was not sure about the influence Angelita wielded over her.

The comtesse had insisted they shopped, making final purchases for the trek, much of which consisted of insect repellents and medical supplies. On the surface, Merran had behaved normally, taking a lively interest in their preparations, but Adrian sensed trouble. He could feel it in his water and it boded ill for the whole expedition.

He shifted his position. The metal surface was growing unbearably hot. The sky was a great arc of azure, the sun a splash of molten gold, unmasked by the tiniest cloud. Adrian grimaced as he thought of the journey ahead, and cursed old man Carter. Had it not been for his – probably senile – whim to send Merran off on this wild-goose chase, they could have been holidaying in Orlando or somewhere equally pleasant where he could have bonked her legless.

And why was Angelita coming along? Adrian wouldn't have thought it her thing, yet she had astounded him by her familiarity with guns, ammunition and other equipment necessary for a sojourn in the wilds. Though he had known her for some years, in the biblical as well as social sense, this was the first time she had displayed this street-wise side of her character. It made him wonder if she had had a misspent youth.

He was becoming suspicious of Miguel, too, disliking the way he monopolised Merran. They spent long hours cooped up together, poring over a tattered map and discussing the contents of a dog-eared book which seemed to be of vital importance. Their conversation always died when Adrian appeared.

Thank God, the farewells seemed to be over. He threw his cigarette to the ground, grinding it into the gravel with the heel of his desert boot, and saying to Merran, 'Are you coming with me? I've not seen you alone for days. D'you want to talk?'

'About what?' she answered flippantly. 'We're only going to catch a plane, Adrian. Not much chance for a heart-to-heart.'

She made certain the chance did not arise during the flight between Rio's Santos Dumont airport and São Paulo's Congonhas field. There the weather was cooler and the rain poured down from the leaden skies with the ferocity of a burst cistern. Whereas Rio was laid-back, São Paulo was committed and dynamic, a magnet for money and talent where skyscrapers dominated the horizon in jagged concrete clusters.

They were met by a fleet of sleek limousines owned by Miguel, and transported to the Brasilton São Paulo Hotel, in which, apparently, he had shares. There was no sign of Nick Slater. In fact, Merran had not set eyes on him since he dropped her off at the villa after that eventful visit to Ipanema. This was an enormous relief – and yet—

'Where's your macho agent?' she asked Miguel when, after dinner, they were seated in the elegant, airy sitting-room of his penthouse suite.

He raised a questioning eyebrow, so distinguished in his custom-made evening jacket that she wondered why she had bothered to look twice at his hired hand, let alone screw him.

'Slater?' he said slowly. 'He's already in Manaus. Why? Have you been misbehaving with him?'

Angelita, in a simple silver slip that reached her thighs, smiled at them demurely. Seated on a couch directly opposite, her feet were tucked under her. Her skirt had ridden up, showing the split crotch scarlet panties that barely covered her mound, framed by black suspenders fastened to sheer silk stockings.

'Kyle told me he saw her with Nick in the early hours

after my party,' she said pointedly, and lifted a tulip-shaped glass of Chablis to her red, cushiony lips.

Miguel fixed Merran with an hypnotic stare. 'Is this true? Consorting with a ruffian? Did you know he's served as a mercenary soldier? A man without honour or principle.'

'He took me to Ipanema – told me about the voodoo ceremonies,' Merran stammered, glad that she was not wearing the amulet. She had wanted to throw it away, but was too superstitious. Instead she had stuffed it in her handbag.

'Is that all? I don't think you're telling the truth,' Miguel persisted. 'Liars need to be punished. Do you think she needs to be punished, Angelita?'

'I do. She must learn to control herself when it comes to men like him,' Angelita agreed, and slipped a hand between her legs, fingernails flashing as the central digit of her right hand began to masturbate her clitoris through the lace-edged slit.

'And what do you suggest?' Miguel's eyes shone as he watched her activity, his iron hand encircling Merran's neck, pulling her slowly towards him.

'Shall we take her into the bedroom?' Angelita murmured, her elegant finger moving faster. Merran found it intensely exciting watching the comtesse pleasuring herself.

'I was planning an early night,' she protested, yet she was overcome by those feelings of guilt and shame that tormented her every time she thought of Nick. 'And I don't like the idea of punishment – sadomasochism has never been my thing.'

'Have you tried it?' Miguel said, his accented voice husky and persuasive, fingertips fluttering over her nipples.

'Well – no – not exactly,' she admitted, spidery tentacles of desire spreading through her belly and breasts until her whole body shivered with need.

'It's a question of contrasts,' he continued softly, finding the dimple at the base of her spine and tracing round it gently. 'One can appreciate a sudden chill on a hot day.' He scooped an ice cube from the wine cooler and dropped it down her cleavage.

Merran yelped.

He chuckled and continued. 'Or the bitter-sweetness of mocha chocolate. The intriguing ambiguity between the taste of tequila and the salt rimming the glass. The angst when one is waiting for a lover to phone. Will he? Won't he? Sex can become humdrum if not kept honed.

The secret lies in the unexpected. Whether to anticipate a caress or a blow. To be strung out on the rack of pleasure, yet unable to satisfy it until your Master says you may. Imagine the ecstasy of release that follows a soupçon of pain.'

He rose, tall and commanding, and drew her up with him. 'There's so much to learn, and I intend to teach you. We are partners, you and I, closer even than lovers, united by a quest. You'll forget Nick Slater and his ilk. They are nothing – crude animals, humping and grinding. They do not understand the finer points of eroticism.'

Above all things she wanted to forget Nick, terrified because he was in her blood.

Angelita and Miguel led her into the bedroom. He sat with her on the wide divan, caressing her breasts and lifting her skirt back over her thighs. She perched on the edge of the bed, her knees apart, and he sank to his heels in front of her, hands stroking the soft inner skin of her legs and pressing the stem of her bud through her satin briefs.

'Lie down, sweetheart,' he crooned. 'That's right. Face down. And then, in a while, I'll bring you to orgasm.'

Tentatively, yet gravid with desire, she stretched out,

her face buried in the cool, herb-scented linen pillow. Miguel lifted her head and slipped a scarf over her eyes, whispering, 'If one can't see, then one's other senses are heightened.'

She felt something soft and silky being knotted round her wrists. Her arms were pulled apart and tethered. Cool air wafted over her buttocks as her skirt was raised waist-high and her panties removed. Her instinct was to close her legs and prevent the exposure of her intimate parts but hands seized her ankles, prising them open and tying them to the footposts.

Silence followed, and Merran's heart raced with anticipation. What were they doing, that demonic pair?

Her nipples felt ultra-sensitive as she pressed them into the quilt. Her clitoris twitched and the velvety walls of her innermost channel pulsed in response.

Her nostrils quivered as a sweet odour penetrated them, pungent, spicy, as strong as opium. Her head spun in the darkness behind her blindfolded eyes. Something touched her between the legs, tickling – teasing. It felt like a feather being drawn over her swollen sex-lips.

This was removed and a furry object circled her anus, then penetrated the entrance of her vulva and hovered there. Pleasure ripped through her body, but it was never allowed satisfaction. She was kept teetering on the edge.

She stirred uneasily, wishing they would untie her and release her from this position of extreme vulnerability. She could smell Angelita's distinct perfume, and guessed that the large finger now rubbing her love-bud belonged to Miguel.

He stroked it, left it before it could explode into joyful orgasm, and massaged each side of it, concentrating on the engorged, unfurled wings. Merran knew she was wet, giving forth that delicious lubrication which no oils on earth could supplant. The rhythmical fondling continued, but no matter how she wriggled, it refused to come into contact with her clitoris.

Without warning his other hand came down across her bottom with a resounding smack. She gasped with shock and indignation.

'You bastard!' she yelled.

'Hush, darling,' he soothed, pinching her desperate clitoris. 'Give yourself up to me.'

He smacked her again and, though it stung, it was bearable. After each blow, he paid attention to her clitoris, subjecting it to the most tender, deliriously pleasurable stimulation. Punishment and reward. The contrast between a smarting, reddening bottom and an achingly sensitive epicentre. In the end she welcomed his blows, begging him to continue, knowing what was to follow.

Perspiration broke out over her skin and she strained against her bonds as her excitement mounted. After one last, hard smack, Miguel frigged her in a quick burst that launched her into climax.

'Ahhh—' she cried. 'Ahhh – God!' And flopped as limp as a rag doll.

She was released, turned on her back, the scarf pulled from her eyes. Half-blinded by the light, she saw Miguel looming above her, his face harsh and set. He hooked her legs over his shoulders and tore open his trousers, then thrust his tumescent organ deep inside her.

'Go on!' Angelita shouted, sprawled on the bed beside them, working a lifelike vibrator in and out of her sex.

He clasped Merran round the hips and pumped vigorously, sending pleasure shooting up through her body. Angelita screamed like a cat on heat as the friction of the imitation penis on her swollen nub brought her to climax. Miguel grunted and reached his goal in a series of spasmodic jerks, and Merran lay under him, spent and exhausted, her juices flowing freely and her bottom on fire.

Nothing had prepared Merran for the flight over the jungle. Hour after hour of crossing a sea of thick vegetation, bright green, sometimes paling slightly only to deepen again.

Here and there appeared an occasional clearing like an island in the middle of an ocean. No roads. No cities. Just an endless emerald carpet embroidered with the silver, threadlike contours of the Amazon's myriad tributaries and then the mighty river itself coming into view. It was no wonder the sailors had once thought it was a sea.

Adrian joined her at the window of Miguel's private plane, staring down and saying, 'It's easy to see why this place draws adventurers, dreamers and romantics. Some stay, others just take a look and move on.'

'It's steeped in legend,' Angelita remarked, glancing up from the poker game she was playing with Liam and Lyn. 'There's one about the river's dolphins. They're supposed to be like mermaids, seducing men, and on nights when the moon's full the males turn into stunningly handsome youths stealing the virtue of every woman they meet.'

'What about the stories of El Dorado, the City of

Gold, and the hidden riches of the Incas? It has inspired explorers down the centuries,' Adrian added. 'Then there are tales of women warriors, and a white-skinned, fair-haired tribe.'

'Even now, when so much of it has been charted?' Merran asked doubtfully, influenced by ecological concern about the rainforests and their inhabitants.

'Even now,' Angelita added mysteriously. 'Who knows what's out there? Treasure? Lost tribes? This is what makes it so interesting.'

The first sight of Manaus was astonishing, a sprawling city built in the densest part of the jungle.

'My grandfather's money helped to do it,' Miguel murmured in Merran's ear as the pilot prepared to land. 'He was a rubber baron. There's even an opera house, dated 1910, and it's recently been reopened.'

They booked in at a five-star hotel ten minutes from the airport. Nick arrived while they were enjoying drinks in the opulent restaurant. He looked scruffier than ever, wearing khaki pants and shirt and a three-day growth of stubble. A floppy-brimmed bush hat part covered his hair. He did not bother to remove it.

Lyn ogled at him and remarked to Merran, 'He's some hunk!'

'You can have him,' Merran muttered, sneaking him a glance then averting her eyes, distressed by her body's responses.

Nick grabbed a chair, spun it round and straddled it, legs spread wide over the seat, tanned forearms folded on the back. Miguel frowned and snapped, 'I didn't send for you.'

'The transport's ready,' Nick informed him curtly. 'We drive to the *estancia* and from there take a launch as far as we can get along the Pican River. After that,' he shrugged his wide shoulders, 'it'll be canoes and on foot. Let's hope there aren't too many rapids. You're entering unmapped regions, Mr Garcia. Have you cleared it with the authorities?'

'Of course.' Miguel looked down his nose as if Nick was a particularly repugnant form of insect.

Nick smiled grimly, and rose slowly to his feet. 'We'll pick you up here at dawn,' he announced, and strode off.

'You look stressed out,' said Liam, catching Merran in the corridor linking their hotel rooms. 'What say we find a bar somewhere and down a few bevvies?'

They took a cab downtown where the port was

crowded with river-boats and jostling humanity. There were caged animals and parrots on sale in the City Market, alongside exotic fruits and vegetables. It was tough, smelly, cosmopolitan and exciting, like no place on earth Merran had ever visited. The atmosphere was vibrant, filled with the babble of a dozen different tongues.

The heat was intense. Within seconds Merran's shirt was sticking to her and sweat ran down her face. They wound up in a shabby quayside bar and sat drinking lukewarm Margaritas.

She relaxed, saying, 'I feel better now I've given the bloodhounds the slip.'

Liam squinted at her through a blue haze of cigarette smoke. 'Garcia?'

'And Slater.' Even to mention his name caused mayhem in her loins. The stickiness of love-juice joined that of sweat between her legs.

'Ah,' he said, and tapped the side of his nose. 'He gets your hormones zinging, doesn't he?'

'I don't know what you mean,' she ground out.

The fan whirred overhead and a prostitute seated on a barstool opened her legs invitingly so Liam could see right up her skirt to where her red sex-lips protruded from a mat of black fuzz. He smiled back at her but shook his head. She prowled off in search of another punter.

'Was I speaking out of turn?' Liam soothed, and placed a hand on Merran's knee. It burned through her jeans, his palm hot and damp. 'We need to get together, two exiles a long way from home. I miss the horses.'

'And I miss Tawstock Grange. Funny, I never used to think about it much when I was away before – but this is different.'

'Let's drink to them.'

They did, often – till a rattling cab spewing exhaust fumes delivered them to the hotel. It was two in the morning, and Merran giggled helplessly as they attempted to creep into her bedroom. There they made love, bedclothes tossed aside in the humidity, which even air-conditioning could not entirely banish.

'Liam,' she whispered, as he came up for air after kissing her mound and parting her labia with his tongue, seeking the pearl hidden within. 'Oh, Liam, d'you remember Mill Street lined with timbered houses, so cool and peaceful by the river?'

'I do. My favourite pub's along there.'

'The Bell and Crown. We drank cider together.'

'And then rode back to the stable and fucked in the hay.'

They fucked now, a gentle, satisfying fuck, nothing kinky – Liam was a straightforward lay. And Merran went to sleep in his arms, dreaming of hedgerows bright with blossom, and *café au lait* cows chewing the cud beneath spreading oak trees.

A transformed Angelita appeared at breakfast. Without Pépé or Raoul or the social scene of Rio she had turned into a female guerrilla leader overnight. It was easy to understand now why the comte had no qualms about letting his lady loose in the jungle.

Her face was wiped clean of make-up, her nails trimmed short and naked of varnish, her hair tied back in a ponytail. It was true that her safari suit was tailor-made, but severely practical nonetheless. She carried an automatic at her left hip and a cartridge belt looped over one shoulder and across her breasts. Merran's libido awoke, stretched and hungered as she watched the comtesse swagger towards the Nissan Patrol like an arrogant young desperado.

The party split up and occupied two vehicles. Miguel and Nick took turns at the wheel of the leading one with

Merran, Angelita and Lyn in the back. One of Angelita's henchmen drove the second, a hulking, shaven-headed prize fighter who answered to the name of Bear. His side-kick, a wiry, one-eyed ugly called Carlos, sat beside him, a rifle across his knees.

Adrian and Liam occupied the back seat amidst the baggage: drip-dry clothes, mountain boots, flashlights, a radio, knives, first aid kits, toilet paper, cameras and plenty of film.

Angelita, checking supplies as they were loaded, had ticked them off on a list. 'Have we plastic bags to store the film? Everything goes mouldy in the damp. Scissors? Yes. Binoculars? OK.'

'My God, anyone would think we're doing a moon landing,' Adrian had commented.

'Don't knock it. You'll be glad I've been so careful,' she had answered sternly, her dominating air acting as an aphrodisiac, arousing lustful images of her cracking a whip.

Later that day Merran leaned her head against the hot leather seat and closed her eyes behind her Ray-Bans. She dozed, then woke after an hour to find the view had not changed, the winding road still hedged in by jungle.

Her shoulder had gone numb with being so long in

the same position. Her head ached as if metal revolved inside it. She passed her tongue over her dry lips and sat up, groaning. Lyn handed her a vacuum flask. Iced orange juice brought relief. She took off the sun-glasses that had made a sweaty ridge on her nose, fluffed out the sides of her hair and stared through the windowless sides of the powerful four-wheel-drive jeep.

'Where are we?' she croaked, lifting the front of her pale blue shirt and blowing down it.

The sweat trickled over her breasts and dripped off her nipples, and her white cotton jeans were too tight round her labia. She regretted not following Angelita's advice and wearing baggy trousers. Even Lyn had left her punky clothes behind, and was as sensibly dressed as the comtesse.

'We'll stay the night at my *estancia*,' Miguel replied over his shoulder. 'It's not far from the river. Not the Amazon, but one of its offshoots. It was there that my grandfather's peons gathered the sap from the rubber trees, boiled up the latex and formed it into balls for shipment down to Manaus.'

'Slave labour,' Nick grunted, his eyes fixed on the road.

'It brought work to the region,' Miguel said coldly, 'and wealth—'

'For some.'

'You're talking crap, Slater,' Angelita butted in with the new aggressiveness that had come with her adoption of masculine gear. 'It made a lot of people stinking rich.'

The atmosphere was charged, and Merran wished she was travelling in the other vehicle. Even Angelita's heavies would be preferable to this. She stared at the road, rutted, swooping and empty. Sometimes the surface was smooth, sometimes pitted and scarred or tortuous, sometimes muddy. Nick's hands gripped the wheel and manoeuvred the sturdy vehicle, a cigarette drooping from between his lips.

It was almost noon, the liquid bubble of sun sucking all life from the earth. The road wound upwards and the trees thinned.

'Get that view!' Lyn exclaimed, leaning forward in her seat.

A fantastic panorama spread out below them, undulating like the sea, shimmering in the heat-haze. Vast stretches of jungle with weird, conical mountains in the distance. Flocks of parrots darted and swooped, and pairs of toucans, beaks almost tumbling them over, drifted across the valley. Then the road snaked round another hairpin bend, becoming an aisle of huge trees.

The sun was at its zenith when they rattled into a village. It was primitive, with no buses, no skyscrapers, no hypermarkets. The whitewashed walls of the tiny church dominated the single square. The bell-tower was gargoyled with black vultures on the lookout for scraps.

'If I don't find a lavatory soon I'm going to wet myself,' Lyn complained as she clambered stiffly down when they parked outside a general store kept by an old woman with a hairy upper lip. Angelita spoke to her in Portuguese.

They were directed to an earth-closet in a hut round the back. It consisted of a hole dug in the ground over which they had to squat. Angelita was in her element, unbuttoning her fly and hitching her pants out of the way while she stood, legs wide apart, directing a stream of urine with as much force as if she was a man.

They went back to the store, sat on the dilapidated verandah and drank tepid red wine while the men went inside to buy more provisions.

Everywhere there was heat and mud and flies. It grated on Merran's nerves; the silence, the mangy dogs, the dirty children and the feeling of being watched.

Nick came out of the building, a cardboard box under

one arm. He seemed taller than ever. The shadow of his hat accentuated the lines of his jaw, the bump of his broken nose, the lean hollows of his cheeks. Sweaty circles spread out under his arms and formed wet patches on his back and chest. His loose pants were tucked into the tops of his boots and he could have been a pirate from any period in history.

Merran tingled with the presage of danger he never failed to evoke and tried not to think of the beast slumbering in his crotch.

Lyn was puzzled by the hostility crackling between them and said, 'This is a spooky place, Nick. And the old cow who minds the shop looks like a witch.'

'You're right.' Merran got to her feet, eager to be in the 4WD again and avoid the desire pumping through her as Nick's eyes scanned her breasts.

With a brow lifted tauntingly, he said, 'You're afraid of the evil-eye, Miss Faulkner? You should wear a *figa*. Didn't you have one once?'

She could feel her cheeks getting hotter. How dare he remind her of the aberration that had taken place on the beach?

'I lost it,' she said, icily.

He clicked his tongue in reproval. 'That's a pity. You

should have hung on to it, for now all the bad luck it warded off will come back on you.'

The road became worse. Miguel had taken the wheel and the rugged vehicle lurched along, hitting potholes. Merran clung to the sides and Lyn clung to her. Angelita seemed unperturbed, even when they approached a bridge over a deep gulley, a fragile looking affair of openwork beams and grass ropes thick as a man's torso. Rocks glistened and foaming white water raced far below them. The planks groaned as, at a snail's pace, they made it across.

'Thank God!' Merran stammered, the sweat running in rivulets from her hairline to her chin.

'Where's your pioneer spirit, Miss Faulkner?' Nick remarked sardonically.

The sky turned a blank grey and the light morbid. Thunder rumbled ominously. The clouds were rent by a jagged fork of lightning, releasing the rain. It fell in a single, unbroken sheet. The travellers were soaked in seconds, water bouncing off the canvas roofs of the Rovers in monumentally large drops.

Moods were low, tempers frayed by the time they reached their destination. Except for Angelita, who seemed to embrace every challenge with open arms.

'Bloody climate!' grumbled Adrian, as they sloshed through the puddles to reach the house, passing a cluster of huts, some covered in corrugated iron, others thatched. All seemed deserted.

The main building was one-storeyed, with a verandah running round three sides. Erected on thick poles, it was reached by a broad, shallow wooden step leading to the front entrance.

'Sweet Jesus Christ!' Adrian continued as Miguel pushed open the door.

'Don't be such a wimp! If you're going to carry on like this then you'd better take one of the Nissans and scuttle back to Manaus,' Angelita snarled, glaring at him as she pushed her way inside and dumped her kitbag.

The rain rattled on the roof as if they were under continual fire.

Bear and Carlos tramped in and out with baggage and found dry kindling. Soon logs blazed in the hearth. Clothes, slung over improvised racks, dried in front of it. A kettle hissed. The smell of coffee raised drooping spirits. Angelita commandeered one of the two bedrooms, stripped off her wet clothes, fastened a sarong around her, and sorted the provisions. Bear, under orders, prepared a meal.

It stopped raining as abruptly as it had started. The sun came out and the jungle steamed. 'There you are, it's not so bad, is it?' Angelita declared triumphantly to all in general, and poured herself a large gin.

Merran lay on a lumpy mattress shrouded in mosquito netting. The women occupied one bedroom, the men the other one, along with the living-quarters. Sleeping-bags had been brought in and hammocks slung between beams. The bed she occupied was big, with room enough for three.

Bear had poked into corners and behind furniture, rooting out insect life that might have taken up residence. Merran was particularly fearful of tarantulas which, according to reports, grew to the size of dinner-plates, devouring small birds and the occasional marmoset. Snakes did not terrify her half as much as spiders, though many could kill at a single strike. The room had proved to be free of such menaces. Even so, she was nervous, the black velvet darkness outside full of alien sounds.

The forest inmates whooped, howled and grunted. It was impossible to sleep and she got up. The sultry night enfolded her like a pall. She lifted her shirt and sprayed her body with a further film of insect repellent.

'If they don't eat you alive, I will,' said Angelita, coming in and openly admiring Merran's nude legs and buttocks.

Lyn followed, carrying a kerosene lamp. This supplemented the single candle. Miguel had promised electricity, but the generator had packed up, as had the shower.

'It's primitive, all right,' Lyn commented, and sat down on a creaky wicker chair to unlace her boots.

'Empty for years, except for fishing trips,' Angelita said, and moved towards Merran. 'I'm enjoying this. Why should men have all the fun? We can play Cowboys and Indians, too.'

'Where are they?' Merran asked, recalling Nick's taut bottom and forceful prick with a sudden rush of lust.

'Oh, drinking, reminiscing – lying about their prowess and the size of their cocks. You know what men are like. They're taking it in turns for sentry duty. Armed to the teeth. I don't know what they expect. The most that will happen is a jaguar or maybe a tapir sniffing around.'

She wore a fresh pair of trousers under a cotton shirt, hardly recognisable as the elegant owner of the Casa Valentine as she checked her revolver before laying it down on the cane dressing-table.

Lyn, boots removed, had shucked off her pants, her tanned skin contrasting with the white cotton briefs she wore. By tacit agreement, they had stored their fancy underwear with the rest of their clothing at the hotel in Manaus, to be collected on the return journey.

All girls together, Merran thought, with a frisson of excitement. She had not felt like that since sleeping in a dormitory at boarding-school. It was there she had first experienced not-so-innocent kisses, soft thighs and breasts and dewy, almost hairless pudenda. There, too, she had discovered the powerful magic of her clitoris, brought to climax by the head girl.

Angelita resembled this forward minx with her tumbling black hair and sparkling violet eyes. But more than that – tonight she seemed to be androgynous – a beautiful creature with a woman's perfect breasts – and—

Glancing down, Merran noticed something odd about the outline of Angelita's fly.

'Ah-ha! I wondered how long it would take you to see it,' the comtesse cried gleefully. 'Treats in store, ladies.'

With tantalising slowness, she unbuttoned her pants and let them slide down her legs, then kicked them away. At first, nothing could be seen, her shirt covering her to mid thigh. She opened it all the way and held it apart.

Merran and Lyn gasped.

She wore a black leather harness strapped round her waist and between her legs. Tailored to fit her body, it was cut high on the thigh to show her shapely brown legs and designed to support a red, penis-shaped dildo that jounced as she walked, a magnificent, nine-inch erection. The illusion that she was some fabulous, twin-sexed being was complete.

She stopped in front of Merran, reached out and rubbed her tingling breasts through the shirt, then started to undo the buttons. When Merran was exposed, Angelita slipped off her shirt and dropped it on the bed. Naked, Merran stared at the fascinating rubber model of a phallus rearing at a ninety-degree angle from the comtesse's pubis. She wanted to slide on to it, to wriggle up and down and see just how far it would sink in until she could take no more.

'You're keen to try it?' Angelita whispered, her warm breath caressing Merran's face as her lips came closer. 'Is this your first time? Are you a virgin who has never been penetrated by a *godemiche* harnessed to a woman?'

She put down a hand and her knuckles brushed Merran's maidenhair and pressed against the tender tip of her clitoris emerging from its soft folds. At the same moment, Angelita's pink tongue stroked across Merran's cheek to her mouth, licked the corner, then the full lips, and very gently parted them.

Merran sighed and opened like a flower to a bee, surrendering to that delicate organ which sipped at and licked and caressed her gums, her teeth, her palate. All the while, the comtesse's finger playfully encouraged Merran's amorous clit, wooing it into stiffness, causing the vital fluid to seep from the sacred entrance to her sex.

Lyn crept closer, her hand cupping her own mound, central finger working busily. Angelita smiled at her. 'You'll not be left out. I'd not leave a sister unsatisfied,' she promised.

Her long fingers continued to play with Merran's bud, now almost overloaded with passion, then she turned round, saying, 'Bend over, darling.'

Merran almost cried out with disappointment, her clit abandoned when it had been on the point of no return. Now she felt the press of the huge latex dildo as Angelita started to ease it into her wet and eager vagina. It filled her. Stretched her. The sensation was strange, for the rubber, though smooth, was chilly, lacking the pulsing blood-flow of the real thing. She had used vibrators, but under her own control. This was like being possessed by a man, yet different.

It warmed in her tunnel, began to feel more natural as the comtesse moved it carefully in and out. Her hands held Merran's breasts so that the aroused nipples poked between her fingers. Lyn positioned herself in front, licking them and the fingers that held them, then going down on her knees, parting Merran's thickened labia and inserting her tongue.

She felt the throb of her excitement growing beneath Lyn's tonguing, intense waves of fire spiralling out from her tiny bud. She arched back against the dildo, determined to ride it, rejoicing to feel Angelita driving it home. Her orgasm started to a peak. She was there, the pulsing, golden sensation roaring through her, a great, searing white light that seemed to go on and on.

She slumped into Lyn's arms, felt Angelita slide from her, was aware of someone settling her on the bed and then saw the comtesse stretched on her back, while Lyn mounted that untiring robot of a prick, wearing the blissful expression which heralded climax. She bucked, erupted, then—

'My turn,' Angelita said, sitting up and removing the harness, the smell of her arousal heady and exotic.

Lyn and Merran became her odalisques, with Lyn concentrating on the iron-hard tips of her nipples, while Merran lowered her face to that hairless pussy where the dark red lips and clitoris were shaped like a butterfly.

'They used to call me Moth Girl,' the comtesse murmured dreamily, lost in sensual pleasure.

Merran's own clit clenched as she remembered Oliver Medway and how he had complimented her on her own beauty. 'Where was this?' she asked, looking up at her from between her legs.

'In the clubs, after I'd run away from convent school. I'll tell you about it one day.'

'It's beautiful,' Merran murmured, supping at the strong, sweet syrup oozing from Angelita's honeyed labia, admiring the gemlike hardness of her sturdy clitoris.

She could feel the heat warming her lower belly again and wanted a second orgasm. The mock penis had not been enough. Her nipples hardened and, even as she stroked the comtesse's clit, her vagina ached to be possessed by a man's power-packed rod.

Chapter Six

The launch was anchored near the jetty below the *estancia*. Named the *Marie Joseph*, she was a two-decker, romantic in appearance and had until not long before been a regular river-boat, plying the Amazon carrying freight and passengers.

Now she belonged to a man called Seth Sullivan, who welcomed the party aboard at first light.

Angelita eyed him as if he was a new stallion in the stable, and Lyn weighed up the possibilities. There was something devilishly attractive about this swashbuckling Irishman, who appeared to be one of Nick's cronies. This fact alone was sufficient to put Merran on her guard and make her immune to his charms.

He was a six-foot-two bull of a man, the left side of his face marked by a thin scar, souvenir of a brawl involving knives. It pulled the corner of his eye a little crooked and lifted his lip into a permanently sceptical expression but detracted not one whit from his overall charisma.

His straggly blond hair was bleached white by the sun, his skin tanned a deep bronze and his eyes a wicked, steely blue-grey. He wore a red plaid shirt, battered jeans, a pair of stout-soled boots, and a large calibre Colt .44 in a holster belted round his hips. This inevitably pushed the formidable bulge between his thighs into prominence.

His crew was led by Juan – stocky with heavy slant-ing eyes that proclaimed Inca ancestry – and Dino – squat, bow-legged, with long, yellowish teeth. Apart from these there were a dozen mestizos, wearing any-thing from shorts to the *cushma*, a smelly, one-piece garment dyed with a solution of mahogany bark and never washed.

These merited hardly a glance, but the two passengers commanded attention. Angelita struck a pose, one hip thrust out, belly sucked in, breasts hard-nippled with interest. Miguel's eyes lingered thoughtfully on the younger of the two.

'I said they could travel with us, Mr Garcia,' Nick informed him as they stood on deck while the sky lightened, brilliant colours fanning out in the east, yellow, fiery orange and shades of mauve.

The jungle presented an innocent aspect as it embraced the brown, fast-flowing river. Parrots chattered as they soared under the forest canopy. Morpho butterflies flitted on electric blue wings, feeding on the nectar oozing from myriad exotic blooms, competing with tiny, whirring humming-birds.

'I should have been consulted,' Miguel demurred, though still undressing the boy with his eyes.

'There was no time. They are botanists, familiar with the terrain and useful with a gun,' Nick said with a shrug, turning away to oversee the loading of gear from the rubber dinghy. 'Don't forget, we'll be living off the land once the supplies start running low.'

'I'm sure they'll be helpful,' Angelita put in, strolling up to the younger, holding out her hand and saying, 'I'm Angelita. What's your name?'

'Estefan,' he replied in a milk chocolate voice that made Merran's toes curl.

What a beautiful plaything, she thought. Supple-bodied, sleek as a cat, he wore check jeans, a blue cotton vest and a mocha-coloured suede jacket. Highly unsuitable for jungle treks, but no matter.

He possessed that incredible grace the Dark Continent bequeaths to all her descendants, no matter how thin the blood is spread. His inky dreadlocks snaked over his shoulders and halfway down his back, and the very air seemed to sizzle around him, projecting lewd images.

'Pleased to meet you, Angelita,' his companion butted in, grinning at her, and his eyes switched to Merran and Lyn. 'Didn't realise we'd have girls aboard. This gets better and better. I'm Terry Clarke.'

His Cockney accent was reassuring, bringing England nearer, and Merran beamed as she shook his hand. He had close-cut hair and a straight, prominent nose, the less handsome of the two but with a potent appeal, all to do with his humorous, vulpine eyes. She sensed he would be ideal to have around in a crisis.

Miguel introduced himself and engaged Estefan in conversation, while Merran and Lyn took Terry to the bar, where they drank like mates of long standing and talked about London non-stop.

Conditions on the *Maria Joseph* were reasonable. She was equipped with staterooms on the upper deck and a galley where meals were prepared. Merran had a cabin to herself, small but clean, with citrus-scented burners plugged into electric wall sockets to discourage mosquitoes. There was a shower with running water, cold and hot, presumably connected to the boiler in the engine room. A vast improvement on the *estancia* where the only way to wash was to stand outside in the rain. The lavatories were not bad either, even if they did flush straight into the river.

'I almost wish I'd a dress so I could change for dinner,' she remarked to Adrian when he carried her bag into the cabin. 'The trip's living up to my expectations, though easy as yet.'

'Just you wait,' he predicted, trying out the narrow wooden bunk. 'I've been mugging up on accounts written by explorers. We can expect jungle, scrub land and impassable mountains. The climate breeds fever and a thousand and one species of hungry insects, mostly on the wing, to say nothing of snakes. There are rivers boiling with rapids, or alive with alligators and piranha fish. And if we go deep, as I suspect Miguel plans to, then we may come across primitive tribes, handy with *curare*-tipped blow-darts.'

'You trying to scare me?' She eyed his well-built body and remembered – oh so much.

The Côte d'Azur and the fun they'd had together. Los Angeles, San Francisco – nights in the gardens of Spain. Hunting at Tawstock, and meets at his family seat in Devon. Varsity balls and English garden parties. Cricket on the village green. A box at the Royal Opera House, Covent Garden. They had almost been a unit, but she had held back from the final commitment, sensible though it had seemed.

He pulled her into his arms so that she lay above him, her thighs pressed to his, her breasts to his chest, his penis burrowing against her belly. 'Darling Merran, I'd never do anything to hurt you. Be sure of that,' he said earnestly, staring up into her wide-spaced amber eyes. 'Why won't you marry me?'

She rested her palms each side of his face, smoothed back the curling fair hair and bent to trace over his lips with the tip of her tongue. 'Not yet,' she murmured, raising herself on her elbows. 'I've not made up my mind if I want to get married. My mother made a mess of it.'

'That doesn't mean you'll do the same.' His hands came up to take the weight of her breasts, naked beneath the cotton shirt.

Merran caught her breath, the strangeness of her surroundings, the steady throb of the *Marie Joseph*'s engine and the powerful thrust of her propeller connecting with every nerve. She needed action, and if not of a violently physical nature, then a sexual one would do.

She moved far enough away to wriggle out of her boots and trousers, then went round on top of him, astride his waist. Still on her knees, she unfastened his shirt and fly. His penis stood up from the opening, firm and satin-skinned, a feast for a hungry woman. With a sigh, Merran lowered herself on the waiting column of flesh. It was rather like going home, familiar and lovely.

She moved her hips up and down, teasing him, lifting her body away so that only her vulva caressed his glans. She hung there, braced on her hands. In vain he tried to push into that elusive place hovering so tantalisingly above him.

Merran laughed, sliding upwards, her wet labia leaving a trail on his chest, then she mounted his face, sinking down so that his mouth corresponded with her lower one. He bit gently at her sex-lips and pulled them. He lapped at her juices, then his tongue fondled her clitoris. Passion surged through her.

He sucked her strongly, his fingers reaching up to flick

at her nipples, driving her into a frenzy. She started to come, her bud flowering, vagina undulating, and he allowed her time, his lips supping off her ambrosial secretions. When the final spasm faded, he moved her down and she poised for a second over his thick penis. He thrust upwards while she squeezed her muscles together hard, aware of his approaching climax, seeing the tortured look on his face and feeling those final convulsions as he, too, reached his nirvana.

'I thought you fancied Angelita,' she said later, as they lay on the single bed in the stuffy cabin.

'I do,' he admitted, cradling her head on his shoulder. 'But she's devoted to Raoul.'

'Really? Not your average Mr and Mrs, surely?'

'Maybe not, but try to part them and you'll find an unexpected solidarity. They suit one another, alike in many ways.'

'She's so tough. I'd never have believed it when we first met.' Merran was remembering the masterful way in which the comtesse had taken her last night.

'She recently told me she ran away from convent school when she was fourteen, lived on her wits in Peru and Colombia, knocked around with the street kids and met Raoul in a bar in Rio,' Adrian said. 'He married her when she was of age. Of course, her family was absolutely acceptable, and she'd done her teenage rebel bit, appreciating luxury again. In fact, she's become greedy. What I'd like to know is, why is she so damned interested in this trip. I've found with Angelita that there's always an element of "what's in it for me?"'

Merran got up and went towards the shower stall. She wanted to tell him the truth but was not sure this was the time. She decided to avoid it for now. 'A whim, I suppose. She seems to be a creature of impulse.' She adroitly changed the subject, running her hands down her thighs and playing with her fleece, adding, 'Why don't you join me in the shower?'

The *Maria Joseph* chugged along steadily, her bow rippling the surface of the river. Seth's sinewy hands rested firmly on the wheel, shirtsleeves rolled up to his elbows, displaying tattooed forearms on which Celtic themes predominated.

'OK so far,' he grunted through the cheroot clamped between his jutting lips.

'You've plenty of supplies aboard?' Nick leaned both arms on the rail. With a sudden glittering cascade of spray, pink-bellied dolphins broke the surface, diving and cavorting, almost taking it upon themselves to act as pilots.

'Sure and I did what you said,' Seth said. 'There's food, fresh water, machetes, ammunition and guns. Quinine, blankets, mosquito nets, fuel and engine spares.'

'I see the canoes roped to the sides.'

'We'll need 'em when we reach the point where the Pican narrows. I'll leave Dino and Juan in charge, and half the men. The rest will go with us.' Seth's eyes slitted as he steered a course round an island of floating logs. 'Not forgetting the "botanists". Garcia didn't argue much, seemed to accept them.'

'We've Estefan's tight little bum to thank for that. Garcia likes them young and pretty,' was Nick's ironic rejoinder. 'The other men? They've had their instructions?'

Seth cast him a glance from under the brim of his wheat-straw hat. 'I don't tell 'em anything. They just do as they're told. Don't worry, Nick. Everything's fine. And that woman?'

'Which one?'

'The one that makes a man's cock leap in his trousers. The tall one, the dark, beautiful one who's playing at being a bloke. I want her.'

'Comtesse Angelita.' The corners of Nick's mouth turned down as he eyed his friend. 'Watch out for her. She's a bitch.'

Seth rumbled with laughter and bared his strong white teeth in a grin. 'All the better. I like bitches.'

'I keep expecting Humphrey Bogart to turn up,' Lyn said at dinner in the saloon that night, a place that had seen better days, though a fan whirred overhead and the food was excellent.

'No, dear, this is South America, not Africa,' Adrian reminded, a brandy glass balanced between his fingers. 'To me it seems more like *Fitzcarraldo*. All we need is a recording of Caruso played on a wind-up gramophone and the illusion would be complete.'

'I hope you'll be able to stand the pace,' Miguel said to Merran later, when they stood aft, smoking and looking out at the ensorcelled night.

It was dark, velvety, rich with the primeval smell of rotting leaf-mould and insectivorous plants. The only light was from the moon and stars. Merran could hear the eerie symphony of the jungle, a swelling crescendo of shrieks, howls, gobblings and the dry, menacing cough of a jaguar on the prowl. It reinforced the sensation that they were indeed in the midst of the world's greatest wilderness.

'I'm not about to lose my nerve,' she said firmly. 'It's a fascinating place.'

His arm came to rest across her shoulders. 'It will get harder when we take to the canoes, but according to your grandfather's map and notes, it shouldn't take us more than a month to reach the mountains.'

'I know. I've read the log, remember,' she said edgily.

Somehow, he and Angelita seemed to have taken everything out of her hands. They were both so dominating. It had become *their* expedition. All right, she conceded that they knew the country, but it was *her* grandfather who had first explored this part of it.

The hands on her back trembled slightly. 'It will be worth it when we find the treasure. Brazil's full of legends telling of jewels and solid gold. The Incas didn't value such things, but their Spanish conquerors did. They took all they could lay their hands on, murdering anyone who denied them. The God-king, the emperor, the last great Inca, is rumoured to have fled from his city and hidden what remained.'

'And if we find it? What then?' Merran asked, telling herself she was being paranoid. Yet she was worried by

Barking and Dagenham Library

E-mail: Libraries@lbbd.gov.uk

Borrowed Items 24/05/2017 18:40
XXXXXXX1045

Item Title	Due Date
* Wild silk	14/06/2017
Search for the truth	03/06/2017
Everything, everything	13/06/2017
Intentions	03/06/2017
Wrecked	03/06/2017
Frisky business	03/06/2017
Run to you	03/06/2017
As weekends go	03/06/2017
With every breath	03/06/2017
Looking inside	03/06/2017
Sun is also a star	03/06/2017

* Indicates items borrowed today
Thankyou for using this unit

www.lbbd.gov.uk/libraries

Miguel's unemotional recital of cruelty and greed that had destroyed a mighty empire and reduced the Inca people to slavery.

His teeth shone in the dark wedge of his face as he said excitedly, 'Then, my darling Merran, we'll take it back to civilisation and sell it to the highest bidder. Undercover, of course – we don't want the South American government involved. This is our secret, Merran, yours and mine and Angelita's. We are the only ones who have copies of the route.'

'While I also have the Brig's notes,' she reminded him, having refused point-blank to let him be the guardian of those. She carried it everywhere, the small journal tucked into her trouser pocket.

'That's true. And this is only fair, but I'm hurt that you did not trust me to Xerox it, as I did the repaired map.'

'It's too old, too frail,' she said, trying to justify her action though telling herself there was no need. She didn't owe Miguel a thing.

'Am I arguing?' His tone was one of bland reasonableness. 'I've a good feeling about this venture. It will make us rich.'

'But you don't need the money. Neither does Angelita, and I certainly don't,' she protested. 'I came because it was the Brig's dying wish. Wouldn't it be better to present the find to the Brazilian nation, to help pay off their crippling debts? I'm sure that's what he intended me to do.'

'I don't think so,' he replied, and the tone of his voice was chilling. 'We shouldn't get any thanks for it. The hoard would probably disappear along the way. There are too many corrupt officials. Trust me, Merran.' He slid an arm round her waist, held her close to his body and bent to kiss her throat, adding, 'You must obey me. I'm your Master.'

This was foreign to Merran's nature. All right, so she could accept a submissive role in the bedroom sometimes, but there it ended. No man told her what to do. And yet he was exciting, this tricky, complicated, devious person, with his aura of wickedness to which everything dark and dangerous within her responded.

'You won't be able to keep it from the others,' she reminded him, while her body quivered as he touched her mound, rubbing where the seam of her slacks pressed between her love-lips. 'You'll need their help to get it to Manaus. They're bound to let the cat out of the bag.'

The deep grooves each side of his mouth accentuated

his sardonic expression. 'All men are venal, my dear – women, too.'

'You're talking bribes?'

'I prefer to call them gifts.'

'And if they won't play ball?'

'That will be too bad. For them, at any rate.'

'What d'you mean?' A bolt of fear shot through Merran and, though she did not withdraw from him physically, her inner self shrank away.

He chuckled and worked a finger deeper into the tight material. 'No need for you to bother your head about details. Leave everything to me.'

She shivered suddenly. 'Let's go inside.'

'You're not feverish, are you?' He was all solicitous concern. 'Are you remembering to take malaria tablets?'

'Yes, yes.' She needed to be with other people, to get away from an atmosphere that hinted at dark alleyways and deceitful dealings.

They rejoined the others, but after a while she noticed that Miguel and Estefan were staring at each other. Miguel slowly ran his tongue round his sensual lower lip. The boy leaned back in his seat, a challenge in his shining black eyes.

Miguel rose and excused himself, leaving the saloon.

Shortly after, Estefan followed. Merran, curiosity and excitement prickling like nettles under her skin, said, 'Oh, dear – I need a tissue. Shan't be a moment,' and skittered out of the door.

The deck was deserted. From somewhere below she could hear an Argentinian tango relayed on a ghetto-blaster. It spoke to the throbbing of her blood. Silently, she made for Miguel's cabin. She crouched by the small round window. He had not bothered to pull the drape across.

They were there, he and Estefan, and the boy was leaning against the wall, his arms stretched languorously above him, watching Miguel, who was slowly unbuttoning the front of his white linen shirt. With each button, he eased back the fabric, revealing more and more of Estefan's smooth, muscular, coffee-coloured chest.

Merran's clitoris spasmed as she saw him lightly cup the boy's breasts as if he were a woman and pinch the nipples till they were erect. He stepped back, looked down and put his hand on Estefan's cock. It strained upwards against his cream chinos. Miguel fell into a rhythm, massaging that hidden phallus. Then he leaned forward and their mouths met, open mouth to open mouth, their tongues flickering and tasting.

Merran's heart was pounding so much she was having trouble breathing. She had seen Miguel fucking Mark at the party, but this was even more exciting as these lovers were unaware they were being watched. Her hand reached into the waistband of her trousers, found it an impediment, unpopped the button and let the zip run all the way down. Never taking her eyes from the men, she pushed the crotch of her panties aside and started to rub her clitoris.

They took off their clothes, unaware of her entranced eyes, naked, powerful and beautiful, two glorious male bodies worshipping one another – and Merran worshipped *them*. Two cocks, hard to bursting, standing up from inky forests of hair. Miguel pulled Estefan closer and kissed him. The boy was shaking with passion.

Merran shook, too, slowed her pace, wanted to make this bubbling excitement last, subjected her eager little nub to slow strokes from above. This way, she could hold on.

Miguel gently laid his lover on the bed, then lowered himself on top, slowly rotating his pelvis.

They smiled into each other's eyes and kissed, mingling their saliva. Miguel turned him over on to his stomach and, after reaching for aromatic oils from the side-table, started to give him a back-rub, hands working all the way down till they caressed his hips and dipped between the taut bottom cheeks.

Merran's breath rushed out of her mouth as she saw him move his index finger into Estefan's hole. She stopped rubbing her swollen clitoris lest it explode with passion. Not yet, she told herself.

She could hear Estefan moaning as he hugged the pillow. Then he turned, and pleaded, 'Suck me, please.'

Miguel went down on him, taking his long thick penis between his lips and sucking vigorously till Estefan bucked and released spurts of semen. Miguel flipped him over again, rolled a condom over his own organ, then eased it between his partner's buttocks and found the tight entrance. The boy pushed against him, aiding his penetration.

At last Miguel's penis disappeared inside and he pumped slowly at first, then faster, and Merran's finger moved in time to his strokes. She could feel herself coming, a massive surge of release sweeping through her as Miguel cried out in ecstasy and slumped on Estefan's back, kissing his neck and murmuring endearments.

*

If I wasn't so lazy and had kept a journal like an earnest Victorian lady traveller, I'd probably find, on looking back, that this was the most pleasant part of the adventure, Merran concluded.

The days passed in somnolent peace, the *Marie Joseph* slipping deeper and deeper into the hinterland. Civilisation simply melted away. Were there such things as television, space travel, war? Only the portable radio kept them in touch, and they hardly bothered to listen to news broadcasts, preferring music channels – the lively, lyrical music of Brazil to which Estefan provided an accompaniment on his guitar.

On and on, a dream river winding ahead, sometimes seen through a veil of rain. 'Now I know how Ulysses must have felt when he was lost at sea, lured on by the song of the sirens,' Merran said to Adrian, lingering on deck during that fleeting quarter-hour dusk, night about to fall as swiftly as a shutter.

'It's getting to you, is it?' he replied with a crooked smile.

'I can't deny it,' and she stretched out her arms, breathing in the air which was laden with the fragrance of distant orchids, knowing she was falling more and more under the spell of the river.

The interlude ended. Next day they entered a lagoon and the only exit was too narrow for the launch to pass through. Seth ordered the anchor to be dropped. The two thirty-foot-long canoes were lowered into the water and loaded to the gunwales with supplies. Oarsmen took their places and the leaders, including Angelita, armed themselves, no one having any illusions about the perils that might lurk round each bend.

Visibility was bad, the rain a grey mist blotting out the forest, hissing on the river's surface, drenching all but those who huddled beneath the palm-thatched awning in the stern. Seth, standing in the prow, a plastic sheet round his hulking shoulders, issued a curt command. In answer the wide, rounded blades of the paddles sliced through the murky water, settling into a steady rhythm.

'This is where we sort the men from the boys,' Angelita commented, lighting up a cigarette. She leaned forward and ran her tongue round the velvety rim of Estefan's ear. 'Are you up to it, *caro mio*?'

The storm passed. The sun shone. A gaggle of scarlet-plumaged birds shot up, screeching as they flew. The jungle was still, yet it radiated colour, lush greens of every hue, and brilliant flowers covering the whole spectrum. Time blurred, but at last they pulled up on a sandbar and prepared to pitch camp.

'Just like being in the Boy Scouts,' Liam said cheerfully, busying himself with getting out essentials from his back-pack.

'Dib dib dib!' Lyn chorused.

'Dob dob dob!' Liam sat on the ground, lit two cigarettes, handed her one and then started to adjust his camera.

'Better keep an eye on your woggle,' she warned. 'This looks just the place to lose it. What d'you think, Estefan?'

'Pardon. I don't understand. What is "woggle"? What is "dib dob"?'

'My goodness, you don't know what you're missing. He'd be a natural for the Scouts, wouldn't he, Miguel?' Lyn teased, very gamine in her safari trouser suit, her hair short and spiky.

The clearing by the river was sandy and hospitable, and the men soon had a blazing fire going. Billy-cans of mate tea and coffee bubbled over the flames. Several crew had gone fishing, and Bear had taken it upon himself to prepare a meal of tinned potatoes and stew, bulked out with pancakes made of cassava flour.

Damn, Merran thought, I need to pee. 'In the bushes,' Angelita said in answer to her query.

This had to be better than the crude facilities on the canoes, where the men stood and made water into the river, or hung their bottoms overboard, and the women were provided with a bucket under the awning. Yet Merran stood there in awe; the bush seemed impenetrable, and who knew what horrors might be hiding in the undergrowth?

'I'll come with you,' Nick said, picking up a machete and hacking away at the lianas blocking the path.

This was embarrassing, but there was no help for it. He was by far the most experienced member of the group, except for Seth, who was fully occupied in setting up camp and organising all-night guard duty, four hours on and four off.

Merran reluctantly followed Nick. The sun shone in burning patches on the mushy ground. The air grew heavier and more humid. Her clothes clung to her like plaster, saturated with sweat. She daydreamed of a bathtub overflowing with warm, scented water. Here deodorants were put to the test. She was sure that she was beginning to smell, even though she had washed out her knickers and T-shirts in the river.

Nick swung the machete easily, cleaved a path and stood aside, pointing out an alcove formed by the massive roots of a huge, vine-covered giant that soared sixty feet. It was a perfect place for her purpose, but even so she ventured within its shelter nervously. This was no English forest where the wildlife was harmless. Here the insects proliferated, growing to nightmare size, flourishing poison sacs and deadly proboscises. They ignored chemical deterrents. Her skin was already covered in puffy blotches from the determined attentions of flies.

Scorpions? Spiders? Fire ants? She lowered her trousers and squatted cautiously, afraid to venture her delicate private parts too close to that leaf-covered soil. This was the kind of predicament guidebooks carefully forgot to mention. But then, this was a part of the jungle where tourists never ventured.

It was a relief to empty her bladder, rearrange her clothing and step out. Nick was leaning against a tree, smoking a thin cheroot.

'Thank you,' she said curtly, trying to forget that she had been watching him all day, aware of his lean flanks and broad shoulders, that hard, beautifully chiselled face, and those piercing eyes which regarded her dispassionately whenever she met them.

She pushed past him, intending to hurry back to camp, but froze when he shouted, 'Don't move!'

An uncanny sound filled the clearing – a curious dry rattling. A sharp retort, and she stared down at the bushmaster writhing in death throes near her feet. She screamed and leapt back, cannoning into Nick. His arms came round her. Her knees gave out and she clung to him, sobbing.

Clouds blanketed the sun. Darkness filled the jungle as rain swept towards them. Nick dragged her into the shelter of the mighty tree again as thunder cracked, the skies opened and the deluge was upon them.

Speechless, Merran stared up into his face. His eyes glittered, his skin shiny with sweat and rain. Unkempt, unshaven, with those hard eyes and cynical smile. But he had rescued her, killed the snake.

'Why didn't you let it bite me? You obviously hate me,' she shouted over the deafening tumult of the storm.

'Maybe I should have done. I warned you to wear the *figa*,' he returned. 'And I don't hate you. You flatter yourself if you think you're that important, but you do represent something I despise. A rich bitch playing games with that scumbag Garcia.'

'You know nothing about me. How dare you be so judgemental?'

'You won't let anyone know you,' he grated, his face pressed close to her ear. His chin was scratchy. It sent tiny shocks down her spine.

'Certainly not an oaf like you,' she hissed in return.

He laughed wolfishly and unfastened his trousers, revealing a splendid erection that sent desire throbbing through her. Before she could move, he pushed her roughly against the tree. The bark dug into her back through her shirt. He grabbed her wrists and held her arms high above her head, his eyes raking over her. Then, with brutal abruptness, his mouth came down to cover hers.

Everything else was wiped out – the rain, the jungle – her fellow explorers. Nothing remained but Nick's mouth. Firm, warm lips surprisingly gentle once they had conquered. Skilful tongue that reasserted its familiarity with the delicate membranes of her mouth. A body honed by hard work, not faddy exercise classes. His chest bruised her breasts, and her nipples crimped beneath that pressure, aching for the touch of his naked flesh.

'Let me go,' she breathed, and the movement of her

hips against the rigid baton of his sex told him she had no intention of trying to escape.

He released one wrist and her hand dived into the opening of his sodden shirt, finding the discs of his nipples and palming them. He groaned, possessed her mouth again as he let go of her other hand, using his own to undo her clothes and expose her breasts. There was an urgency about him which fanned her desire.

She stood, legs apart, her back supported by the tree as he forced her trousers down over her hips, then found her mound, impatiently pushing the panties aside, his fingers entering the soft, warm wetness of her cleft. His mouth was arousing her beyond control, and the touch of his slippery finger on her clitoris was enough to tip her over the edge. The feeling rippled through her loins, cold as ice, hot as fire, rushing to her brain and exploding in a firework display.

'Now I'm going to fuck you,' Nick growled, while the rain beat down even more fiercely and the thunder pounded, making the forest shake.

Their clothing was in the way, but he lifted her, his hands supporting her under her bottom. He did not guide his penis but prodded blindly between her legs, finding her swollen entrance and thrusting in all the way.

Her hungry vagina took the length and width of him, convulsing round it.

'Yes,' she moaned. 'Oh, yes. Do it, Nick.'

He held her tightly, clutching at her haunches, taking her weight as he glared into her face, growling, 'I'm going to fuck you harder than you've ever been fucked.'

He withdrew his stiff cock and then plunged it back into her with all his strength. She groaned with pleasure, feeling it filling her completely, almost hurting her with its size.

He snarled and pistoned into her again and again, as if his phallus was a machine, made of metal not flesh. She knotted her fingers in his streaming hair and clamped her mouth over his, giving strange, shuddering cries. Nick punished her with his penis, grunting as he took her.

This isn't love, she thought while thought was at all possible. It isn't even sex as humans know it. This is raw, animal mating, as these creatures all around us in the jungle mate.

He built up speed and she bit at his lips in the intensity of her pleasure. He was slapping against her, thrusting wildly, working his cock in and out with such savage strength that tears of pain and pleasure rolled down her cheeks. And then he tore his mouth free, flung back his head and bared his teeth as his body shuddered with the ferocity of his crisis.

Merran hung there, speared on his prick, rejoicing to feel it twitching inside her with the throbbing urgency of coming. Every trace of sophistication had vanished, replaced by a primitive being rejoicing at being used by her mate – the strongest male in the pack.

Slowly he released her and her trembling legs nearly buckled beneath her as her feet contacted the marshy carpet. His penis slipped out, leaving her bereft. They did not speak, a strange spell holding them.

She pulled up her trousers and fastened them. So did he. Retrieving her hat, he plonked it on her head. She did not even bother to thank him. The storm passed. The sky cleared. The sun began to bake everything again. It was time for them to return.

Chapter Seven

Well, Brig I hope you're satisfied, Merran thought wryly. If this was your idea of a joke, then I don't get it. But if, however, you intended the experience should be an enlightening one, then you've certainly succeeded.

Oliver Medway's words in his surgery that wintry evening now seemed prophetic. How long ago was it? A lifetime or more?

At first it had seemed like an adventure, to be undertaken light-heartedly. Then she had been able to appreciate the beauty of the river as they paddled past jungle-clad islands and large black boulders jutting out from the swirling waters. Steep hillsides rose on either bank, raucous macaws flew overhead, and they had negotiated little channels full of exotic scents, butterflies and flowers. There had been lovely campsites on rocky inlets with mica-strewn beaches.

But further upstream conditions had deteriorated, with the river meandering through a curtain of dripping trees and lianas. It was sluggish and treacherous. With hardly any warning it could turn into a series of rushing, perilous rapids. Then portage was the only way forward. Everything was taken from the canoes and carried further along the bank to where the water became calmer, the boats themselves manhandled by way of winches and ropes.

'I'm sick of being a pack mule,' Merran announced bitterly after a week of hard slog when they had met one rapid after another.

Her feet were sore, chafed by her constantly soggy boots. Her skin itched from insect bites. Her clothes were torn, sweaty and damp. The sun either scorched them unmercifully or became obscured by a low ceiling of cloud. Often the rain came down with a relentless force that went on for hours.

Food was getting short; they had lost valuable supplies during one particularly hazardous portage. Game seemed to have vanished from the swampy landscape and fish had become their staple diet.

'What I'd give for a bacon butty,' Lyn said longingly as they chewed on an unappetising mess of rice and grilled pirarucu, having just set up camp after another exhausting day.

'I'd settle for a burger bar,' Liam answered, his face streaked with mud. 'I once avoided them like the plague, but now – give me a Big Mac, French fries and a chocolate milkshake.'

'Or a cup of tea made with water that isn't laced with chloride,' Merran sighed.

'Alligator meat's tasty, but they're tricky to shoot. The buggers just slide into the water if disturbed and then you've lost 'em,' Seth put in, wreathed in cheroot smoke to fend off the flies. 'Monkey isn't bad. A bit stringy.'

Merran shuddered. 'How could you? They're like us.'

He fixed her with a flinty stare. 'I guess we'd eat each other if we were starving.'

She realised he was serious and, resting back on her elbows, glanced furtively round at her companions. They had changed dramatically. The men had given up the struggle to shave, each developing a beard and moustache. They were all thinner. The rainforest was steadily reducing them to a bunch of ragged scarecrows. Once the idea would have been laughable, but now cannibalism was not beyond the realms of possibility.

'I'm tired of listening to you grumbling,' Angelita said pithily, stretching like a cat and looking round the group in search of tonight's star prize. The harsh conditions seemed to suit her, sexual appetite in no way impaired. She was the only one not troubled by mosquitoes. 'We've food in our bellies, haven't we? OK, so it's not a gourmet's delight, but it keeps us going.'

'Going where,' Adrian growled, already swinging in his hammock, swathed in netting like a giant chrysalid.

'Going forward. We're almost there. I can smell it in the air,' declared Miguel, fingers tracing over the map, eyes glittering feverishly in the firelight.

'And where's that, Mr Garcia?' Nick was polishing his single-barrelled 20-gauge shotgun with an oiled rag, fighting the erosion that ate into anything metallic.

He had become even more morose and, along with Seth, spent most of his time trying to prevent the oarsmen stealing more than their fair share of the rations. A thankless task, judging by the rapidity with which the stores were diminishing.

It was as if a shutter dropped down over Miguel's

face. 'To our destination, Slater,' he snapped, and thrust the map into his pocket.

'Destination?' Nick's eyes were like spears. 'Oh, so there is one? You told me this was a sight-seeing trip.'

'So it is – that's right – to visit Inca ruins.'

'That's the first I've heard of it.' Nick, cleaning completed, raised the gun and sighted down the barrel at Miguel. He lowered it, but continued to search his boss's face. 'I don't think you've been quite honest with me, Mr Garcia.'

Merran stared at him, as fascinated as a rabbit with a snake. Nick had become more masterful as they penetrated deeper into the wilderness, a born leader with Seth as his second-in-command. Terry had toughened up, too, and she was sure he was something other than a botanist. As for Estefan? Miguel's catamite he might be, but he acted like an experienced campaigner. Who were these men? Friend or foe?

Though Merran had feared Nick might try to repeat the intimacy they had shared, this had not happened. He avoided her except when strictly necessary. For her own satisfaction, and also to spite him, she had seized any opportunity that presented itself to screw Adrian, Liam and Miguel.

Each man fulfilled different aspects of her needs, one tender and friendly, the other a jokey companion. Miguel dominated her, using her to appease his own peculiar hungers, unleashing the dark side of her nature. The things he did to her would have seemed weird and kinky not so long ago. Now she found that she needed punishment, subconsciously weighed down by a load of guilt because she enjoyed sex without love.

The hectic fertility of the jungle aroused her unbearably. Everywhere she looked there were plants that resembled phalli or pudenda, some flaunting enormous trumpet-like flowers with bulging stamens exhaling stinks that intoxicated the pollen-carrying insects. The humid air was heavy with the smell of death and decaying vegetation, mingled with sweet, unexpected stabs of fragance. It was violent, shocking, fantastic and compelling, a weird nightmare of a place.

'*Les Fleurs du Mal*,' she said to Adrian one evening when they were seeking a place in which to fornicate. 'I keep thinking of Baudelaire's poems.'

'*Flowers of Evil*. My dear Merran, you always did suffer from an overactive imagination. Plants are plants, that's all,' he had responded, already unzipping his trousers. 'You wouldn't get all steamed up in the sedate sanctity of Kew Gardens, would you?'

'Don't patronise me,' she had snapped, but held the thick, hot rod of his penis in her hand, unable to resist the sexual urge which seemed out of control lately.

Now she was prepared to turn in, but as she left the perimeter of the woods after performing necessary bodily functions, someone stepped out from behind a tree, barring her way.

'I want to talk to you, Merran,' Miguel said.

'God! You made me jump. Don't creep up on me like that!' she shouted irritably.

His lips curled in a sneer. 'Frightened, are we? You said you wouldn't lose your nerve.'

'I haven't,' she vowed, getting a grip on her emotions, aware of acute disappointment. It was shaming to admit, even to herself, that she had hoped it was Nick.

'I know,' he whispered soothingly, and his arm slipped round her waist, hauling her against his hard muscled body. 'I'm proud of you.'

Above all things she craved approval, and relaxed in his arms. Her nipples felt tender, rubbed by her linen shirt. They ached for caresses, and Miguel sensed their need, slipping a hand through the button front, cupping one breast and letting his thumb brush over the tip.

Merran arched her back and closed her eyes, a moan escaping her lips. Locked together as they were in lust, she felt the quivering readiness of his cock trapped fully erect inside his trousers. He kissed her, his black beard abrasive, yet exciting. His tongue performed a dance of desire, coiling with hers, sending electric shocks winging to her loins. He moved down over her chin, to lick her neck and lap at the hollow of her throat where a pulse throbbed. Every millimetre of her skin responded, tinglingly alive.

She thrust her hips at him, overwhelmed with desire. His hands slipped to her belt, released it and opened her trousers, and she hurried to help him. He slipped his fingers between her thighs, entering the wet delta of her sex. She opened her legs and he rubbed his thumb-pad teasingly over the turgid head of her clitoris, then suddenly stopped.

'Go on,' she pleaded huskily. 'Please – please—'

'Not here. I want to make love to you properly,' he whispered, and she held her trousers up with one hand as he took the other and led her to the deserted river bank. There he spread his combat jacket on the sand.

She lay down and held out her arms to him. The heavens were ablaze, the sky clear and star-filled, comets shooting across the indigo vault of the cosmos. Merran gave herself up to the beauty of the magical night, Miguel a part of it, sombre, mysterious, bringing unbridled rapture to her body and senses.

He undressed her as carefully as if she was a treasure of incalculable value. 'That's lovely,' she murmured as the breeze rippled over her skin. 'It's so long since I've been naked. I've not dared, because of the mosquitoes.'

'They aren't here tonight,' he said. 'Maybe there's something they don't like. A river plant perhaps.'

He lay beside her, his hands and lips performing ancient rites, his fingers sliding deep in her sex till she cried out sharply into his mouth. He took off his boots and trousers and, shirt open over his hairy chest and belly, moved round to kneel between her legs.

'Play with your nipples,' he ordered. 'Make them stand up in peaks while I watch you.'

She clasped a hand round each full orb and fondled the swollen teats, lightly pinching them, the rushing sensation of pleasure echoed in her thrumming bud. 'I want to come,' she whimpered.

'I know you do, but first you must serve me.'

He was over her now, straddling her chest with his strong thighs, guiding his engorged prick into her mouth. Merran worked her tongue over the silky shaft, feeling the glans poking the back of her throat. He took his weight on his braced arms, thrusting in and out as if he was penetrating her vagina.

She could not move, wedged between him and the sand, and he took his pleasure of her mouth but stopped before he ejaculated. He slid down her body and nudged her knees apart, then thrust into her molten depths, again and again till she felt him convulse in orgasm.

She wound her legs round him, ankles crossed over his buttocks, surrendering to his passion. He was her Master, and other men paled in comparison – save for one, and she quickly blanked her mind to the memory of him.

Miguel hung above her for a moment, then rolled to one side and skimmed a hand over her prone body, finding the avenue between her wide-spread legs, circling the tight mouth of her anus and fondling her eager clitoris. She gasped, rocked against his fingers, and he took her up and up till she came, crying out with the pleasure of it.

He patted her mons and sat up. She lay with an arm

flung over her eyes, but was aware of his movements as he reached for his jacket. The sudden glare of a flashlight brought her out of her satiated trance.

'Let me see your grandfather's log,' he said urgently. 'Judging by the map, we've nearly reached the spot where we must leave the river and go inland. I need to check this.'

She struggled into a sitting position, found her trousers and took the small book from one of the numerous pockets. Miguel scanned it, the torch in one hand, its beam running over the closely written pages.

The magic had abruptly vanished. Now she was aware of rustlings in the bushes and the calls of nightjars. She started to pull on her clothes, needing something between herself and the hundred and one predators waiting to suck her blood. Only by using insect spray all over before dressing was it possible to repel the hungry little winged creatures, so small yet so deadly.

'Can you find the place?' she asked, curling closer to Miguel's side, suddenly scared. 'Are we almost there?'

'Not yet,' he said slowly. 'But when we strike into the jungle, I think we'll eventually find the mountains.'

'The Brig gave up before this happened,' she reminded, and doom settled over her soul. 'His party were too ill and weak to continue. One of them was bitten by a fer-der-lance and died horribly in great agony.'

'I know, but it was forty years ago. We are better equipped and medicine has advanced. We'll find the relics. I'm certain of it.' His voice was harsh, his face oddly lit by the upward beam of the flashlight, showing harsh cheekbones, long nose, deep pits of eye-sockets.

Merran experienced the chilling certainty that he had sought her out with more than sex in mind. He wanted to enslave her body and subject her will to his. She was important to him while she had the log in her possession. What would happen if and when they found the treasure?

'She's randy as a bitch on heat, but close as a clam,' Seth muttered as he changed watch with Nick at midnight. 'I've screwed the arse off her, but she never says a thing about where we're bloody going, or why. As for getting a peep at the map – forget it.'

'I'm sure it's a chore for you, shagging Angelita,' Nick answered with a grin, hefting his rifle and preparing to retire to his hammock.

'Oh, it is, but I was never one to shirk duty,' the Irishman said solemnly, his eyes twinkling. 'And

Estefan's had no better luck with Garcia. Those two don't mix business with pleasure.'

'It doesn't matter. Let them lead us to the treasure, if in fact it exists, and then we'll go into action,' Nick assured him, clapped him on the shoulder and slipped away through the woods, seeming to float soundlessly over the ground.

Seth settled his back against the bole of a tree and lit a cheroot. The crack of a branch underfoot told him that Angelita was on her way. He smiled grimly, opened his fly and massaged his penis, sliding back the foreskin, his fingers already slippery. It was huge, throbbing and ready when she pounced on him like a succubus intent on draining him of his vital substances.

They had gone as far as they could by water, now coming to ravines where the rapids boiled and churned. 'We'll leave the canoes here,' Miguel said decisively, adding aside to Merran, 'I believe this is where your grandfather abandoned his boats, continuing on foot.'

The canoes were hidden in the scrub with several men left to guard them, and the equipment loaded into packs. Merran staggered under the weight of the heavy knapsack as Liam helped her hoist it over her shoulders. Seth, Nick and Miguel were consulting compasses, and Miguel had reluctantly allowed them a cursory glance at the map.

'Are you sure you want to go on, Mr Garcia?' Nick said seriously. 'It seems a damned dangerous trip just to look at a few crumbling monuments.'

'There's no question about it,' Miguel rapped out, his hand coming to rest on the butt of his pistol. 'We go on.'

'OK, though you do realise that this part of Brazil is still mainly unexplored?' Nick warned, screwing up his eyes and staring at the sun, taking a bearing. 'If we head north we should locate the mountains.'

For days they struggled through spongy forest and over slimy rocks thick with moss, moving slowly forward in a perpetual dim green light. Occasional rays pierced the canopy, where orchids, passion flowers and creepers grew a hundred feet overhead.

The jungle was claustrophobic, hot and steamy. Long beards of greyish vine hanging serpent-like from branches conveyed an air of menace. At times the density opened out to flat swampland, broken here and there with little islands and thickets of bamboo.

'Snakes' favourite places,' Nick informed Merran.

'Watch your step. I might not be there with a gun next time you meet one.'

He seemed to be in his element, stripped down to a pair of cut-offs and stout boots, his broad chest glistening with sweat. Sometimes he would grab up his gun, stuff his pockets with cartridges and set off, returning more often than not with a bush turkey or a young tapir. Then Bear would get a fire alight and they'd eat, fresh meat a relief from manioc flour mixed with condensed milk.

The way became steeper and they reached a wall of massive rock with thick jungle converging at its base. A waterfall gushed from on high, tumbling down the sheer face of a precipice. Dropping their packs, the whole party ran towards it.

Merran's throat was parched, her body prickling with heat, and she dropped to her knees, plunging her hands and head into the icy torrent, letting it soak into her clothes. Blessed water, fresh and clean. Nothing had ever tasted half as good.

She looked up and met Nick's eyes across the fine mist flung up by the cascade. He stared at her unblinkingly, a wild man of the woods. His hair and beard dripped, and water ran in rivulets across his arms and torso, saturating his shorts so they clung to his genitals.

I hate him, she told herself. He's mean and untrustworthy.

She tossed back her hair and went off to examine the terrain with Angelita. It was dim in the gully, the sides of the strange, conical escarpment rearing aloft, fleeced with greenery and pitted with caves.

'I'll bet it's got a flat top,' Angelita exclaimed. 'Doesn't it remind you of the mountain in *Close Encounters*?'

'It's higher than it looks,' Lyn added, as they followed the rugged path. 'D'you suppose the Inca remains are near here?'

'I don't know,' Merran answered truthfully, though she had a tingling in the tips of her fingers, almost a foreknowledge that left her with a not-quite-sane, other-worldly feeling. Perhaps I'm feverish, she thought.

On all sides was a wild confusion of tumbled boulders and tangled vegetation. Estefan was enraptured by the gorgeous butterflies dipping over the water. They were yellow and grey, with hind wings ending in dark brown tails.

It was like entering an earthly paradise. They wandered on, lured by the clear warble of a bell-bird, finally reaching a pool into which the fall plummeted. It sparkled, bubbled and frothed, promising cool delight. Angelita started to strip, shouting, 'Let's swim!'

Soon she was thigh-deep in the amber, slow-running water, looking like Venus herself, classic as a marble statue from a king's palace. Her voluptuous buttocks were stippled with goose-pimples, her nipples standing proud from the dark brown areolae, her pubis a sharp wedge of black fluff, no longer depilated.

She and Lyn sank with little screams into the stream where an overhanging branch provided protective shade. Out in the full glare, Merran rinsed her clothes and spread them to dry. She waded back in, the cold silk sand flowing from under her soles, burying her to the ankles.

Estefan was romping with the others, diving, ducking, splashing. Merran plunged in, swimming strongly, then floating on her back. The pool was enchanting. There would be no anacondas, piranhas, weeds or unnameable dangers lurking in its depths. Angelita swam towards her, limbs flashing, hair flowing. With a wide smile, she slid her slippery arms round her, holding her close as their feet touched the bottom.

Lyn, lithe and boyish, yielded her body to their caresses, while Estefan circled round, admiring them but having no inclination to join in.

'Haven't you ever had a woman?' Angelita asked him, her breasts bobbing where the water cut across them.

'No,' he answered cheerfully, dark skin covered in myriad diamond drops. 'I tried once, but it was like making love to another female, almost lesbian. I couldn't get a hard-on. We spent the night playing Scrabble and giggling and comparing notes about the men in our lives and what bastards they were.'

'It's such a waste,' Angelita lamented. 'You're so stunning.'

She urged Merran towards the waterfall. They shrieked as the deluge broke over them, though Angelita's shoulders took the full force. Her hands were on Merran's buttocks, going between the tight crease, touching the plump secret lips, while spray stung their uplifted faces.

'It's so cold,' Merran cried, freeing herself and making for the bank where she stood shivering and gulping air.

'Too hot. Too cold. This is a country of harsh contrasts,' Estefan said, wading towards her, shaking his dreadlocks, naked and godlike and beautiful.

Then everything happened at once. The trees and bushes formed into human shapes. Merran was suddenly ringed by stocky warriors with brown skins dyed in red and ochre patterns, glossy coal-black hair cut pudding-basin style, lips distended by discs and noses pierced with porcupine quills.

Gesticulating and gabbling excitedly, several flourished long spears. Others splashed into the pool and pulled Angelita and Lyn to the bank. Their touch was not hurtful, more curious and pleased as they handled breasts and dived their fingers between thighs. Estefan seemed to fascinate them, and he stood motionless, permitting any liberty they cared to take as they examined his penis and testicles and the tiny eyelet of his back passage.

He addressed them in several languages, then gave up, shouting across to Merran, 'They don't understand me, only a word or two here and there. I don't think they'll harm us.'

She pointed towards her clothes, and one of the braves smiled over sharply filed teeth, and nodded his head, but when she went to put them on, he prevented her. The other men picked up all the clothing strewn on the bank and carried it over their arms, laughing and exclaiming. They were completely naked, their bodies smooth-skinned and almost hairless. Short of stature, they had lean hips and tight buttocks, and penises that bounced as they walked.

Still jabbering, curious, lively, seeming to find the

situation amusing, they prodded their captives gently in the backs, indicating that they were to go with them. Panicking, Merran looked wildly round her, but Angelita said, 'Don't even try it. Escape is impossible. Now, at any rate. Do as they want.'

'No doubt they've been watching us ever since we arrived. These people are adapted to the jungle. They move silently, have their own codes of conduct,' Estefan said as they walked between a guard of warriors.

'You know a lot about it,' Lyn remarked, eyeing one particularly good-looking young buck. 'How come? I thought you were only interested in flora and fauna and fucking men.'

'I've studied the Forest Indians,' he replied, almost off-handedly. 'It's a great pity they will eventually become extinct.'

Merran was causing the most excitement among the braves. They seemed unable to resist touching her hair as it dried out, lightening and curling, flowing like a silken mantle over her shoulders.

'Why me?' she murmured, embarrassed by so much attention.

'Maybe they've never seen a white woman before,' Estefan suggested.

'Angelita and Lyn are white,' she averred.

'Yes, but being blond, you must seem like a goddess.'

'Maybe they think you'll taste better than the rest of us,' Angelita put in, looking longingly at her revolver and cartridge belt which was way out of reach, borne along with the rest of their clothes.

'Not cannibals?' Merran's sphincter clenched with fear.

'Headhunters perhaps,' Angelita went on. 'And I'm not talking recruitment executives.'

'Oh my God,' Lyn whimpered.

After what seemed an endless trek across warm humus, the woods opened out into a large clearing dotted with palm-thatched huts. The tribe gathered, leaving their cooking-fires and dwellings and running towards the hunting-party.

'We should have brought presents for them,' Estefan said.

'We weren't exactly expecting this,' Angelita reminded him sarcastically.

The tribe formed a circle round them and the warriors stood back, preening themselves and obviously being showered with praise. Merran followed Estefan and Angelita's example and made no protest as the women and children touched her. These were a handsome people, some naked, others wearing brief loincloths, their brown skin having an attractive sheen, their profiles almost Egyptian, their long, stalk-straight hair cut with fringes over their foreheads.

Then the crowd parted, making way for a strange-looking figure. He was older than the rest, and his bright, intelligent eyes fastened on Merran. She stared back, concealing her unease.

His high-cheekboned face was painted in square patterns with berry juice. He wore a shirt of woven grass with a design worked on it in purple dye. A headdress of animal hide topped his grizzled hair. His neck and chest were covered in necklaces of small stones and jaguar teeth. Quills decked with bright feathers pierced his ears.

He paced round the newcomers, sniffing the air and rattling a seed-filled gourd.

'The shaman,' Estefan said, and stepped forward to greet him. He bowed and, after unbuckling his wrist-watch, presented it to the medicine man.

A murmur arose from the onlookers, their faces wreathed in smiles, black eyes shining. The shaman took the watch, examining the digital face. Estefan showed him how to attach it to his wrist and the man nodded, took off a leather string from which there hung a large flat pebble etched with symbols and slipped it over Estefan's head. Then he started to speak, pointing at Merran with a gnarled, brown finger, the clawlike nail bearing a half-moon of dirt.

A chill ran down her spine. She could not understand a word but sensed that it concerned her. Estefan listened and nodded, then answered in the same tongue, translating for his companions.

'He says we are welcome. We shall be their guests. He is particularly interested in Merran. He wants her to accompany the women and allow herself to be prepared.'

'What for?' she gasped, her knees turning to water, all the stories she had ever heard about human sacrifice rising to the surface of her mind. She didn't fancy pouring out her blood on their altar to appease the gods.

Estefan exchanged more words with the shaman, then turned back to her. 'It's all right. There's nothing to fear. He wants to present you to their chief. Go along with it, Merran. May as well humour the old guy. After all, you've no alternative, have you?'

'Tell him Lyn and I insist on going with her,' Angelita said belligerently. 'And we want our clothes back.'

Estefan frowned slightly. 'OK, but whatever you do, don't use your gun. These are peacable people.'

The shaman issued curt instructions to half a dozen of the youngest women, and Merran was led away to one of the huts. Its dimness enfolded her and she was thankful. Angelita might not mind being the focus of so many eyes, but she certainly did not enjoy it.

The interior was clean, and light filtered through the crudely constructed windows. The women had brought in their clothes, laying them on a palliasse balanced on four short wooden feet. A frame of branches and lianas formed a base, covered by a mattress of leaves.

Merran reached for her trousers, but the leader of the women, a raven-haired beauty whose skin had the bloom of a Victoria plum, placed gentle fingers on her arm and shook her head. At her order, the others carried in calabashes filled with water and the ritual of washing and grooming began.

Merran received the most attention. She was examined from head to toe. The leader took one of her breasts in her hand and lifted it. The sensation was far from unpleasant, and when she bent and sucked at the nipple, shocks of desire speared Merran's womb and she could feel her lower self becoming wet.

A swift glance over the girl's head showed her that Lyn and Angelita were also being caressed by their dusky-skinned attendants. Merran's paramour looked up with a smile, then explored further, her tongue diving down to probe into her navel, while her fingers fondled the fair bush covering her mound.

Merran stood there, awash with desire and throbbing anticipation. The women came round and supported her from behind, reaching under her armpits and stroking her nipples. An agonised, delirious ache radiated from those tormented crests to the hard bud of her clitoris.

Now the beautiful Indian parted Merran's labia, her head cocked to one side as she stared admiringly at the tea-rose pink hue of those delicate lips. She beckoned her companions to join her in the examination of Merran's female parts. Then she took off the strip of cloth that covered her own genitals and opened her legs wide, reaching down to tangle with her wiry pubic hair and stretch wide her labia majora. Her inner lips shone between the swelling outer pair, and her clitoris was large, standing up stiffly.

Merran experienced a spasm of voluptuous pleasure that wrenched her cervix and made her moist inside. No wonder they were so much in awe of her pink membranes. The native girl's parts were very pronounced, the lips of a bluish black colour. Merran could smell her, an acrid odour like ebony wood soaked in sea-water. She groaned, admitting her need, and the hands continued to tweak and rouse her nipples while the girl sank to her knees, parted Merran's swollen wings and sank a finger into the wetness of her vagina.

Merran's head went back and her throat arched. 'Oh – oh—' she whispered, and her hands rested on her female lover's head, urging her on.

The fingers continued to play with her puckered teats, while the girl caressed her clit with a firm tongue-tip, and then sucked it into her mouth, rolling it beneath her tongue. Merran was in ecstasy: never had she been given such superb cunnilingus.

Through half-closed eyes she could see Lyn and Angelita on the palliasse, brought to the same stage of bliss by their attendants. The sight of her friends being pleasured fanned the fires of her lust and she could feel herself reaching that point where nothing could prevent her precious orgasm or interrupt that mad plunge towards fulfilment. Her clitoris felt like an enormous bud ready to burst into bloom.

The girl sucked harder. The tongue worked busily. The

fingers flicked at Merran's nipples and, with a loud cry, she came in a welter of pleasure that left her trembling.

Her lover smiled and murmured, reaching up to kiss her. Merran could smell and taste herself on those brown lips and, in a daze, permitted the women to wash her and anoint her with perfumed oils. Her hair was combed and then one of the more mature ones brought in a long cloak made of bird-of-paradise feathers and laid it carefully over Merran's shoulders. 'Darling, how sumptuous!' exclaimed Angelita, sprawled on the leafy mattress, her legs wide open, a native girl subjecting her to caresses. 'I hope they give one to me.'

Estefan, still nude, came to the hut door and said to Merran, 'They're getting a feast ready, but first you have to meet the chief. Go with the shaman, and don't be afraid.'

This is crazy, she kept thinking as she followed the old sorcerer across the compound, where everyone watched her closely. It's like a scene from the *Royal Hunt of the Sun*. I'm dreaming, surely.

No dream. They arrived at the largest of the huts and the shaman stood back so that she might step inside. There, half blinded by the contrast between the gloom and the bright golden light outside, Merran paused.

And then she saw him.

He was seated on a throne-like wooden chair, and she found herself coming under the appraisal of the bluest eyes that she had ever seen. He rose, a perfect specimen of European manhood. Gigantic of stature, strapping and broad-shouldered, his skin was like bronze and his mane of hair flaxen.

'Hello,' she cried, the relief of seeing a white man making her forget that he might expect some sort of protocol. 'What a relief that you're in charge. Perhaps you can help us find our friends. We wandered off and got lost.'

He smiled and shook his head, gesturing in bewilderment. Her heart sank. He did not speak English. She tried French and Spanish to no avail. He continued to smile with lips that were finely chiselled and sensitive.

She could almost hear Lyn exclaiming, 'What a babe!'

They were alone in the hut and he came towards her, put out a hand and touched her breasts. His eyes were large and alert and so very blue, and Merran leaned towards him, her body moving of its own volition. What woman would not respond to such a magnificent young savage?

Questions flooded her mind. How had he come to be

there and how long had he been their chief – and why? Just for the moment she didn't care, everything else seeming insignificant against her raging desire to have him fill her vagina with his cock.

He unfastened the leather thong which was all he wore and his penis sprang free, fully erect, rearing up to touch his navel. It was pale-skinned, scored with blue veins, the bulging glans twin-lobed and glossy. As if having a life of its own, it thrust out from the fair thicket of his underbelly while his hand went to his balls, testing their weight, fondling them, preparing them for the task ahead.

'You want me?' she asked, thinking: That's a daft question when the answer's apparent. She could not wait to have that huge member sinking into the heartland of her sex.

'Eh?' Puzzlement clouded his eyes, and his big hand pushed aside the feathered cloak and reached round to hold one of her buttocks, sliding the fingers between them and then pulling her hard against his mighty phallus.

Her breath shortened and the juices bedewing her pussy-lips increased to a warm, wet flood. She would need all the lubrication she could get to help fit his organ within her, and was glad the native girl had already brought her to climax.

'Can't you even tell me your name?' she insisted, smelling the rich odour of his clean, naked flesh and the warm, musky essence rising from his splendid equipment.

'Name?' he repeated, and his fair brows drew together in a frown as if he struggled to capture a fleeting memory.

'I'm Merran,' she said, and a video flickered across the screen of her brain. An old black and white movie and a hunk in a leather loincloth saying: 'Me Tarzan. You Jane'.

Why bother to talk when all they both wanted was sex? she wondered, but pressed a finger to his broad, hairless chest, asking, 'Who are you?'

Daylight dawned. His eyes lit up. 'Ah,' he said, and tapped himself. 'Jon.'

'Jon?' she repeated, liking the sound of it.

'Jon,' he affirmed, and then went on to tell her things in that impossibly obscure language.

She placed her fingers over his lips, silencing him. His fleshy tongue came out to lick them, and a shiver went all the way up her arm, across her shoulders, down her spine and settled in her clitoris.

'Nice name,' she whispered and, confident that he could not understand a word, added, 'Nice cock. I want to play with it, Jon.'

She replaced her fingers with her lips, kissing his mouth, inserting her tongue inside and feeling his instant response, white-hot lights flashing in her head. He grunted, captured one of her thighs between his, rubbed his penis up and down against her, primitive, unschooled, excitingly needful.

He sank with her to the carpet of leaves that covered the floor, the great feathered cloak billowing beneath them, bright, so bright, in vibrant reds and acid yellows, neon greens and Stygian black. Civilisation melted away. She wanted nothing but this man – the leader, the chief, he of the highest rank – and she was his Chosen One. His mate.

No foreplay. Nothing but Jon's great curving cock plunging into her till it seemed he would penetrate her very heart. His eyes flashed and he thrust harder, and she reached down and stroked her clitoris in rhythm to his thrusts. Her fingers smeared her juices over his stem and then back up to the hard ridge of her engorged bud.

She moved faster, circling, rubbing, and he moaned as they started their mutual journey towards oblivion.

Beneath her fingers she was close to orgasm, and their touch on the root of his cock spurred him onwards. He bucked like a rampant stallion, and she rode the spiralling intensity of their passion till her climax thundered through her.

Then Jon cried out, the pumping motion of his hips rising to a frenzy His cock jerked, he sank his teeth into her neck and she felt him quiver with the violence of release.

Chapter Eight

'Where the hell are they?' Nick snarled, more worried than he was prepared to admit.

His concern was not so much for the others; it was Merran who had got under his skin, that annoying woman with her feisty foolhardiness and unforgettable body. Throughout the trip he had had to keep his distance from her or carry a permanent erection around with him.

She had been missing for three hours. Adrian and Liam had scoured the surrounding area and come back with long faces and nothing to report. They were fretting and wanted to organise a proper search party. Miguel seemed unperturbed, seated by the waterfall and staring up at the mountain in absorbed fascination.

'The comtesse won't take unnecessary risks. I expect she's exploring the caves,' he said calmly.

'That's not good enough,' Adrian declared, haggard and unkempt, a far cry from the playboy who had once been the debs' delight.

Liam took a nervous drag at a cigarette. 'Sure it isn't,' he agreed. 'We should do something about it right now.'

Nick clenched his fist and mastered the urge to take Miguel by the throat and choke the life out of him. 'Supposing one of them has had an accident,' he pointed out.

'There were four, weren't there? Someone would have got back and raised the alarm,' Miguel returned, levelling him a venomous look. 'We can't waste time because of them. I'm telling you, the comtesse will take care of everything.'

'Your trust in her is quite touching,' Seth commented heavily. 'But why did she go off? She should know the rules about keeping together.'

'She's a law unto herself,' Miguel grated, his face like thunder. 'They'll find the way back. Meanwhile, we'll pack up what's needed, leave the rest of the stuff here, and start climbing.'

'Not me. I'm going to look for them,' Nick said stubbornly.

'You were hired to obey orders,' Miguel cracked out, pulling rank.

'Who's going to stop me? You?' Nick's voice was colder than permafrost on the tundra. He stepped closer, thrusting his bearded face into Miguel's.

Behind him he could hear the Garcia henchmen closing ranks, Bear and Carlos and the rest. He agreed with Seth that these men were a liability, loud-mouthed and unstable, always blasting away with their rifles, wasting ammunition and scaring off more game than they caught. Trust the Don to employ cut-throats as his personal army. He was glad he had brought several of his own stalwarts along. At least he could rely on them, each one a fully trained fighter.

'Are you following this madman's example, Sullivan?' Miguel answered, a muscle twitching at the side of his mouth.

Seth cast an eye round the camp, fished a cheroot from his pocket and stuck it in his mouth. 'I don't feel right about leaving the women,' he growled as he lit it. 'Reckon I'll go along with Nick.'

'Me, too,' said Terry, his eyes razor-keen. 'We need to

get a bearing, Nick. You're the most experienced climber.'

The jungle was vast and uncharted. There was nothing for it but scaling the rockface to get the lie of the land. Nick set out, nimble as a chamois, finding hand-holds and toe-holes and sensible flattish bits, going higher till the canopy lay below him, an unbroken sea of green.

He stood on a promontory, shading his eyes with his hand. The sun drew up a vapour of heat. A condor soared effortlessly on the thermals and the long clear cry of the lemon-coloured ventevea rang out. A flock of olive-brown amarillos rose in flight, disturbed by his presence, uttering a confused chorus of notes.

It was impossible to stand there and doubt the existence of a creative force. Nick was awed by the magnificence of the almost primordial vista, fearing for it, wanting to protect it.

His attention was suddenly captured by a thin column of smoke rising through the trees in the far distance. Where there was smoke would be fire, and this meant habitation. The only people that lived in such a wild and remote region were Forest Indians.

He scrambled down the steep slopes and reported his

find to Seth and Terry, Adrian and Liam. Within half an hour they were off, packs on their backs and guns primed. Miguel watched them go with cold eyes, then ordered his men to load up and begin the perilous ascent to the nearest cave.

Merran stirred, dazed with sleep, the leafy mattress rustling under her. She was at once aware of strange odours, strange light, a strange male body curled, spoon-fashion, against her back.

Then she remembered: she was in a hut in the Amazonian jungle and had been fucking a tribal chieftain who, in keeping with this insane, Alice-in-Wonderland world, happened to be white.

She could feel his stiff penis resting between her thighs, the bulging glans nudging against her anus. She was sticky from their last coupling, the afternoon having passed in a haze of passion. She had lost count of the number of times she had climaxed.

Jon was remarkable, so male, so animal, so beautiful, a veritable Adonis. Merran turned in his arms and found that he was awake and looking at her with those inno-cent, childlike eyes. Dear God, she thought, I could love this man.

He touched her cheek with his finger, softly, tentatively, and the ice in which she had deliberately encapsulated her heart was beginning to melt away. Nick had started the process, and Jon had very nearly completed it. It hurt to feel so vulnerable.

Then he smiled, and she came to the conclusion that perhaps this was the perfect relationship – no words to come between them, no sarcasm, mixed messages, lies – just the language of the flesh. And yet – she liked to talk, sparking off from another person's ideas. Communication was vital. Could she really live without that?

Jon drew her to him, stroking her breasts and the damp hair coating her mons. She grasped his phallus, testing its size in her fist, sliding up and down along its length, seeing the purplish glans poking between her fingers. At first he had proved inept in bringing her to climax, but she had found satisfaction in teaching him the refinements of love-making, almost as if she was initiating a virgin. And now she stopped him when he wanted to insert his cock into her entrance without foreplay.

'No, Jon, not yet,' she whispered, though knowing he would not understand her. 'I want to come first. I showed you how. Remember?'

She rolled on her back, raised her knees and opened her legs. The rosy petals of her sex unfurled, fringed by golden-brown fuzz. She dipped a finger into her vulva and spread the clear fluid over her cleft and up across the cowl of her clitoris. The tiny organ swelled and emerged and she held her labia apart.

Jon slithered down till he sat between her legs. His fingers joined hers, and having guided him to her pleasure-centre, she lifted her hands and fondled her nipples. He stared down at the fascinating display of delicate moist membrane, rubbing one big, blunt-ended digit over her clit.

The sensation was exquisite, rippling up to her breasts. 'Lick it,' Merran moaned, and grasped the back of his neck, pushing him down on her.

He feasted on her honey-dew, and she could feel that large slippery tongue working diligently. More exciting still, he took his mouth away so he might examine her passion-bud, watching it in wonder. Merran wanted more and urged him to stretch out on the primitive couch. Then, supple as a cat, she wriggled round till she rested across his body, her lips fastening on his massive shaft. He sighed with pleasure and buried his face between her legs, lifting her to his mouth again.

She inhaled his scent, and felt his tongue plunging inside her as she closed her lips round the top of his penis, tasting the salty, pungent juice. Her hand caressed the soft skin of his balls, nails scratching lightly at the sensitive area dividing them from his nether hole.

She sucked with abandon, taking his prick from her mouth to lick across its slit lasciviously, inserting the tip of her tongue into it. Jon bucked, quivered, but did not come. He was concentrating on giving her delight, his tongue flicking against her anguished clit. It was too much to bear. Passion poured through her and she groaned helplessly, mouth locked around his penis.

It was coming. There was no stopping it. A mist enfolded her brain, and the annihilating storm of orgasm tossed her high and racked her body with violent spasms.

Jon seized her while she lay convulsed, and with frantic haste turned her so he could thrust into her body, rocking against her with blunt, hard strokes, spearing her with his weapon. He came almost at once, crying out with joy.

Merran was flattened beneath him, his head on her shoulder, his long hair tangling with hers. Her body was wet with sweat and saliva and love-juices. Her vulva was sore from the penetration of his thick member, yet she had never felt more tranquil. This was life at its simplest. No worries about tomorrow. Just the here and now.

She came to herself, aware of someone in the hut. The shaman hovered over them, outlandish in his animal skins, necklaces clicking like agitated bats. Estefan was with him.

'There's a kind of glorified barbecue waiting. No sausages, I'm afraid, but lots of other goodies. You're the guest of honour,' he informed her, black eyes twinkling.

He was wearing his shirt and boots but no trousers. The shaman kept touching him, sliding a hand round his muscular rump and fingering the channel between.

'Why have they selected me?' she asked huskily, realising how sweet it was to hear a human voice again.

'Ah, thereby hangs a tale,' Estefan answered mysteriously. 'I've been cross-questioning our friendly medicine man.'

'He fancies you,' she said with a laugh, sitting up while Jon lounged beside her, supremely content, judging by his wide smile.

'Who doesn't?' Estefan joked, then he sobered. 'Didn't you wonder how a white guy happens to be their honcho?'

'Of course, but then I forgot. We've been busy.'

'So I see.' He sat on the side of the palliasse, his shirt falling open. His long, purple-dark penis jutted forward and the shaman looked at it and licked his lips.

'Well,' Estefan continued, 'it seems Baby Jon was found toddling in the forest about twenty years ago. The tribe adopted him after they found his dead parents.'

'OK. So why make him king?'

'Legend had it that a golden-haired god was coming to them, bringing a thousand years of peace and plenty.'

'Was there nothing to prove his identity?' Poor child, she was thinking, poor, frightened little boy 'Yes, but the Indians can't read and have their own obscure lingo. We're lucky the shaman has mixed with other tribes and that he and I hit on a kind of mutual jungle-speak. He has shown me the few things found in Jon's parents' camp. According to a battered diary, they were English anthropologists, but went down with malaria. They didn't stand a hope in hell. There are a few snapshots of Jon with his father and beautiful blonde mother. When you turned up, the tribe thought she had been reborn. His sacred mother-bride. That's why you're the flavour of the month.'

'You're putting me on, aren't you?' Merran sat there stunned, holding Jon's hand and pressing it to her breast, awash with pity and tenderness.

'Not me, honey.'

'He'll want me to stay as his wife?'

'He already has four, and several kids, but, yes – I guess that's the general idea.'

'What do we do?'

'Play it by ear.'

'Are they friendly? Have they treated you well?'

'Couldn't be better,' Estefan smiled. 'I haven't had such a ball since I left Los Angeles. Most of these guys are bi. And the shaman isn't greedy – more than willing to share me.'

'And what about Angelita and Lyn?'

'They can take their pick, and these people are so handsome. The comtesse thinks she's died and gone straight to heaven.'

'Will they let us go?'

'Do we want to?' Estefan shrugged his broad shoulders and flicked back his locks. The shaman flung him a smile of besotted admiration.

'I don't think I'd like to be cut off from civilisation forever.' Now that Merran had recovered from the carnal madness that had obsessed her all afternoon, she was beginning to weigh up the pros and cons.

'I'm not so sure.' Estefan was receiving the shaman's homage without moving a muscle, as the older man knelt between his spread knees and worshipped at the font of his sex. 'No wars, no money troubles – no homophobia.'

'No shops, no movies – no music! I couldn't live without music,' she cried.

'They have their own. Listen,' Estefan said dreamily, his eyes heavy-lidded as the shaman sucked his penis vigorously.

She could hear it – wailing flutes and throbbing drums – like bird calls and thunder. The song of the jungle.

The down rose on her limbs and she shivered, surrendering to it, as Estefan surrendered to the shaman. He came into his mouth in a milky volley that trickled over the medicine man's chin and dripped down to mingle with the jaguar-fang necklace.

Great fires blazed, throwing up sparks into the brief twilight, and the tribe gathered to dance and eat and drink, celebrating the arrival of their goddess. Their bodies shone, their night-black hair gleamed, their skins were bright with dyes, shells, flowers and feathers.

Merran's nostrils quivered in response to the odour of roast sucking-pig. Her stomach rumbled. She was starving. The women stirred the cooking-pots filled with chunks of fish and vegetables. They were merry, chattering ceaselessly, peeping shyly at her.

Jon sat on the ground with the elders and indicated that she take her place beside him. She had put on the feathered cloak again, and that was all she wore. This way, she was constantly available any time he wanted to finger her, or insert his penis in her body or between the valley of her breasts.

The meal was set before them, and the women carried in calabashes containing liquor made from fermented cassava roots. 'Treat it with respect,' Estefan warned. 'It's got a kick like a mule.'

The beer circulated. The pipes trilled and dark fingers beat a tattoo on taut drumskins. Angelita weaved to her feet and started to dance in the middle of the circle. She wore nothing but a pair of white panties, the triangular shadow of her pubic hair showing through the fabric. Her big breasts jiggled as she moved. She cupped them in her hands and made the nipples harden and prick up.

One of the natives joined her, posturing and gyrating lewdly. He grabbed her round the waist, pumping his pubis against hers, his tool pointing towards the moon.

She shrieked and leapt high. He caught and held her, tore off her panties and speared her while she continued screeching like an alleycat on heat. He bent her backwards, still skewered on his prick, and her legs clamped round him in a scissor-lock. The crowd cheered, and couples began to pair off.

The elders sat, eyes slitted, backs straight, in a trance after sniffing at a dark brown substance the shaman took from his pouch. He seemed possessed of an animal spirit, pawing the dust and chasing Estefan, who pretended to be his prey.

Everywhere Merran looked people were joined together. The firelight played over shining brown bodies linked by mouths or genitals, a tangle of limbs, a hump-backed beast or daisy-chain. The tribe had no inhibitions, openly enjoying the varied delights of sexual congress.

Lyn lay with an Indian between her legs, his hands busy at her clitoris. She looked relaxed and happy as he drew up her knees and sheathed himself in her welcoming wetness. Angelita, having wandered away from the circle, was on the ground with two supple, raven-haired nymphets. One was tonguing her love-bud, the other positioned on her face, while Angelita lapped at the slate-blue lips so generously parted that she might enjoy their special flavour.

Jon, who had been drinking, kissed Merran thoroughly, chewing at her tongue, eating her teeth and gums. Then he took up one of the ripe fruits from the platter in front of him and, holding her down, began to push it into her vagina. It split, pips and juice running into her channel and across her thighs. The sensation was exciting, sticky, cool, as wet and slushy as snow in sunlight.

She laughed up into his handsome face as he leaned over her and slowly, inch by delicious inch, eased his erection into her till she was full of his turgid prick and pulped fruit. She squirmed, sighed, gave herself up to the pleasure of his fingers smearing her love-bud with juice, skimming over it, back and forth, till she erupted into orgasm.

Then he was on her, pumping and grinding. Her loins responded to his violent thrusts and everything seemed to burst asunder as his seed shot out, filling her with his ecstasy.

As she floated down from the heavenly spheres to which he had carried her, she opened her eyes and saw Nick Slater striding into the clearing.

The warriors got themselves together with remarkable speed. One moment they were screwing anything that breathed, the next they were on their feet, armed and facing the intruders. Jon extricated himself from Merran and leapt up, his face expressing amazement as he stared at men with skins similar to his own. The elders woke. The shaman crouched, shaking his beaded rattle. Nick signalled to his companions to stand back and, unarmed, walked into the circle. He dropped his knapsack to the floor, opened it, and rummaged through the contents.

Dozens of pairs of eyes watched him suspiciously. Without making any comment concerning Jon's colouring, he handed him a Swiss Army knife, and demonstrated its gadgets. Once they saw their chief accept both the gift and the strangers, the tribe congregated round them.

The shaman received a shaving mirror, and the women murmured in appreciation of the bundle of red cotton cloth produced. Plastic beads proved popular, and combs, too, along with badges and buttons. Nick had selected handouts before he left Manaus, well aware that gifts usually built bridges and prevented bloodshed.

Merran huddled inside the cloak, waiting events. Obviously the situation was a delicate one, and the tribe must be propitiated. Angelita and Lyn drew close, for once silent and watchful.

'Nick's a party-pooper,' Angelita commented.

'I'm glad to see him,' Lyn replied, pressing up against Merran as if needing reassurance. 'I don't want to be stuck here for ever. I need shops and a town.'

Merran was confused. Part of her had almost come to accept that tribal living was now her lot. Jon had filled her horizon and she had begun to visualise staying with him for good, learning jungle lore, bearing his children, watching them grow like young saplings, uncorrupted by the wicked world as she knew it.

The shaman smiled. Jon smiled, too. On cue, the women handed hollowed gourds of cassava beer to the newcomers. 'Good Lord, it tastes like rum,' Adrian pronounced, and the tension broke into laughter.

Seth swept Angelita into a bearhug. Lyn was carried off into the bushes by Terry. Liam was pounced upon by a lithe Indian maiden who proceeded to strip off his trousers, and Adrian enfolded Merran in an embrace.

The tribe, no way deterred by this influx of visitors, returned to the simple pleasures of fornication, encouraging them to join in.

Only Nick remained aloof, making sure that a couple of his followers mounted guard on the edge of the camp, and then going into a huddle with the shaman, Estefan and Jon.

It's just like him to come barging in and spoil everything, Merran thought, her spirits sinking. For some unaccountable reason she wanted to cry.

The orgy went on till the last reveller slept, exhausted. Merran crept to Jon's hut alone. He squatted on his hunkers by the fire, drinking with his newfound white brothers, while Estefan and the shaman translated and Nick illustrated the conversation with pictures drawn in the dust with a pointed stick. It was as if Merran no longer existed for any of them.

Men! she thought crossly. They're all the same. If it isn't football it's golf, or model trains or planes or racing cars. They never grow up. My mother could not accept this. I can. Let them play. Women have a more important role. Peter Pan and Wendy. Wasn't she the one who mothered the Lost Boys?

On this superior note, she washed away the residue of mashed fruit and lust, climbed on to the palliasse and dragged the woven blanket over her. Mosquitoes whined and, cursing, she jumped up and sprayed herself with the last remaining drops of repellent from her bag. Perhaps the shaman would give her something to keep the infuriating little pests away. If they stayed, that was. What did Nick have in mind? And where was Miguel?

'Oh, Grandfather,' she wailed. 'Why did you do this to me?'

She slept fitfully and was awakened by a fearful noise. It seemed to come from all around her. A loud, clear cry rising to a blood-curdling scream. Before it died, it was joined by a booming chorus. Merran ran out of the hut. The bushes close by shook and the roaring went on. The leaves parted on a simian face with a wide open mouth. She sighed with relief. It was nothing more harmful than a group of howler-monkeys greeting the day.

The stars went out as she watched. A pale pink film stretched over the sky, and it was cold. She shivered, aware of her nakedness, turning back to the hut and walking into Nick. His arms came about her and he let her cry on his shoulder. She cried for a long time, and rubbed her wet face against his shirt.

'Hey, your nose is snotty,' he complained, a thread of amusement running through his voice. 'What's up, Miss Faulkner?'

'Nothing.' She pulled away from him, dragging the back of her hand across her nose.

'It's a pretty big sort of nothing to get to a hard lady like you,' he commented.

'Just shut up and give me a cigarette.'

'I'll share one with you. We're running out fast. Aren't you going to invite me into your little wooden hut?'

'It's not mine. It's Jon's,' she said sulkily, wanting to kick herself for showing weakness, and to him of all people.

'I thought you were Queen of the Jungle round here,' he said with a quirky, sarcastic smile. 'Now you've had his pecker up your fanny.'

He was crude, scruffy and bearded, his shorts torn, his shirt ragged, yet she loved his deep drawl and wanted him to go on talking, talking, as if he would never stop.

'Come on in, then,' she said, and lifted aside the curtain that hung over the entrance. 'Sorry I can't offer you anything.'

'What, no gin and tonic? Haven't you had time to

drop down to the drugstore? How remiss, Mrs Jungle Jon.'

'Get lost.'

'Don't worry. I've brought my own,' he said, and produced a half bottle of whisky from one of the capacious pockets of his bush jacket. He took a slug, then passed it to her, adding, 'Here's mud in your eye.'

They sat on the bed and he told her about Miguel, and all that had taken place. He also said he had convinced the shaman and Jon that she wasn't a goddess, simply a traveller who had got lost. They had agreed to let her go. He had enlisted their aid in finding whatever it was Miguel sought.

He shot her a sharp green-eyed stare, face close to hers as he added, 'What is it, Merran? Won't you tell me what all this is about?'

She shifted uneasily, too aware of the proximity of his hands, his mouth, his cock. 'I don't know if I can trust you.'

'Thanks a bunch. You trusted that rattlesnake Garcia.'

'All right. Maybe I was wrong. I don't know what to believe any more.' Her lips trembled and she was losing her grip again.

'Take a chance on me,' he whispered, and pulled her

to him between his bare muscular thighs, nuzzling her throat.

'Oh, Nick.' She was trying to be sensible but her wits seemed to have deserted her. With a mighty effort, she broke from him and fetched the log and map. 'Here. You'd better read this, but Miguel will be angry if he finds out I've told you.'

'Miguel's a rat. He doesn't own you, does he?' His eyes contained chips of green ice. 'OK, so he may have introduced you to SM, tied you up, spanked your ass, but you're your own person, Merran, for fuck's sake.'

She was speechless for a second, then, 'How did you know?' she breathed, her cheeks flaming.

'I know everything,' he said, then grinned. 'Least ways, I thought I did, but this log now – that's something else.'

He stretched on the bed, propped himself up on one elbow and started to read. Merran, tired of standing, lay beside him, curled up against his back. He reached over with his free hand and ran his fingers absentmindedly across her breasts and belly, then toyed with her pussy, reading all the while.

Heaviness invaded her womb and she waited in breathless anticipation, wanting, hoping, longing for him to touch the fulcrum of her pleasure. She did not have to wait long.

'Humm, this is real interesting,' he said, his eyes running across the pages. 'Your Granddaddy was certainly some guy.'

'He was,' she croaked, lifting her pubis towards those tantalising fingers.

Casually he touched that miraculous little pearl at the top of her cleft. She drew in a sharp breath as, still concentrating on the reading matter, he stroked it, very gently. Merran stayed quiet, afraid to move lest that caress be withdrawn. It wasn't.

Nick subjected her to sweet, uncomplicated masturbation, a persistent massage of her clitoris that silenced her, deepened her breathing and dropped her into a deep pool of contemplation. It was nearly as good as when she did it to herself. Without pausing in his reading, he brought her to a shattering climax.

Then he laid the book aside, turned to her and she saw his prick distending the leg of his shorts, the end poking through the denim fringe, a tear at its single eye. Her hands tugged at his belt. The shorts came down, were kicked aside, and he straddled her, looking deeply into her eyes and saying, 'Watch me when I go into you.'

He took the thick shaft in his hand and ran its head over her sensitised labia, then lowered himself a little, pushing against her entrance. She watched, seeing it being absorbed into her body. He grabbed her round the hips, and thrust deeper so that she could no longer see what was happening, didn't want to, her eyes shut as she held on tight while they surfed the crashing wave of bliss.

'It's just as we thought,' Nick opined, throwing himself down on the turf beneath a clump of shady thorns, the sunlight falling through the leaves and making patterns on his face.

'How so?' Seth glanced across at him, honing his bowie knife on a stone.

'I've read the log kept by Brigadier Carter.'

'She let you see it, then, did she? What did you have to do? Fuck her?'

'Yep, but she'd have shown it to me anyway. The lady's scared.'

'So, your little whore was right? The obliging Carmensita.'

'She's a useful grass, and Garcia was careless, inviting the Rio tarts to orgies. Loose talk, Seth – invaluable to us.'

'Carmensita loves you, Nick.'

'Maybe. I haven't time to get mixed up in love.'

Seth eyed him sceptically, took a gulp of cassava beer, tossed it around his palate and spat it out. He shuddered. 'That's pretty rough stuff. Like the poteen we used to make back in Killarney I woke up with one hell of a hangover.' He took another pull, swallowing it this time. 'So, where do we go from here?'

'Treasure-hunting.'

Progress was easier, for now they had the natives to help them. Jon was in the lead, eager to show the way, though the shaman had shaken his head and prophesied doom if they angered the gods by tampering with such a holy place. Jon had shouted him down, the advent of his own kind making him rebellious. The shaman had shrugged, looked at Estefan, and decided to go along.

Jon took them by a different route, a short cut to the base of the mountain. They climbed steadily, the trees thinning, and eventually reached a large fissure that penetrated deeply into the rocks. 'We'll stay here tonight,' Nick pronounced, and had everyone collecting brushwood.

It was a sober party who huddled round the fire. The

Indians were uneasy, frightened of ghosts, of demons and of the bats that had swarmed from the caves in their thousands when darkness came, great black swooping phalanxes in search of food.

There was no sign of Miguel. 'Where is he?' Angelita asked anxiously.

'Who knows? In the caves higher up, I shouldn't wonder,' Merran answered without much conviction.

She had sunk into herself, wanting no one, wrapped in her jacket by the cave entrance, staring at the mesmeric flames. Outside the glow of firelight the jungle was filled with the rustlings of hidden hunting creatures. She thought she would never sleep, but woke hours later aware of warmth at her back. Nick sat there, long legs stretched out and crossed at the ankles, hat pulled over his eyes, a rifle across his knees. He grinned at her.

'Good morning, Miss Faulkner.'

She did not reply, moving her cramped limbs awkwardly, then standing and spreading her arms wide. The sun came up over the ridge and dried the dew. The scene was grand, wild and rugged. The noise of animal life increased. A posse of parakeets rocketed out of the foliage and zoomed across the clearing.

'How beautiful it is,' she whispered.

'You can say that again,' Nick answered, coming to standing at her side. 'It's terrible, remorseless and magnificent. Once you've been here, it never lets you go. You can try to stay away, but it draws you back.'

'Did it do that to you?' He's a strange man, she was thinking, made up of so many different facets.

'Yep.'

'Is that why you came on the trip?'

'One of the reasons.' His eyes were unfathomable, and his firm mouth captivated her. She wanted to kiss him, to feel those lips feeding on her.

It was then that Miguel suddenly appeared from the cave. He looked so strange that everyone fell silent. Then he saw Angelita and hurried towards her. 'Darling, there you are. I've found it.'

'The treasure?' she asked, going into his arms, gazing up into his feverish eyes.

'Sshh!' he exclaimed. 'This is for you alone.'

'I think not,' Nick said crisply and Miguel spun round, hand flying to his gun and half drawing it from the holster.

'Mind your own business, Slater,' he shouted. 'Don't try to follow us or I'll shoot.'

'He's not joking,' muttered Seth, knuckling the sleep from his eyes.

The commotion woke the others. Adrian and Liam reached for their rifles. Estefan and Terry came awake at once, as soldiers will. Jon's fist closed round his spear. The only one who missed the action was Lyn, curled up in her sleeping-bag like a baby.

Merran stepped forward. 'Can't I come, Miguel?' she asked, thinking: Humour him. He's mad.

He hesitated, scowling at her. Merran threw a look of appeal at Angelita who seemed very worried, her eyes searching Miguel's face anxiously, as if the adventure was getting out of hand and taking an unexpectedly serious turn.

'Merran is one of us, darling,' she murmured. 'You are her Master, too.'

He did not answer, his eyes like burning pits in his cadaverous face. He was shaking and pouring sweat.

'Be careful,' Nick hissed in Merran's ear. 'His men should be somewhere around.'

'I'm going with him,' she replied, keeping her voice low. 'Don't be far behind will you?'

'Bet your sweet life I won't,' he assured her, squeezing her hand. 'When we get out of this, I'm going to take

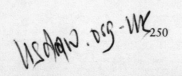

250

you to a five-star hotel and spend a week between the sheets, screwing you legless.'

'I may just keep you to that.'

She walked up to Miguel and he led her into the cave. Soon it became necessary to use flashlamps as darkness settled around them, a thick darkness filled with the choking smell of bat droppings. The floor was sandy and strewn with boulders. It sloped upwards and Merran could feel the chill of fear crawling down her spine.

Was Nick following? She dared not look round.

Chapter Nine

Miguel seemed able to see in the dark, but the women stumbled. 'For God's sake, use your torch,' Angelita shouted, her voice bouncing off the walls.

He stopped so abruptly that they cannoned into him, with Angelita swearing and Merran afraid to move lest some horror should pounce on her from the inky blackness.

The flashlight's beam struck glistening wet rock and a tunnel that disappeared ahead. It was narrow and shale-strewn, twisting and turning, gradually ascending, a tortuous climb that seemed to go on for ever. The silence was broken only by the drip, drip of water. Then, without warning, Miguel stepped out on to a wide ledge.

'Look!' he cried, with the triumphant air of a magician producing a rabbit from a hat. 'Isn't it stupendous?'

They stood in an amphitheatre the size of a football-pitch. Though Miguel's men had stuck flares in niches the ruddy, flickering light was lost in the gloom of its seemingly endless roof. It struck awe into Merran, this cathedral built by nature for the worship of – what?'

Angelita recovered first, facetiously dismissive. 'It's grand, *caro,* absolutely, but where's the bar?'

'All I can offer you is coffee,' he said with a sinister smile. 'But once we've shipped back my find, you'll be able to buy up every bar in Rio, and then some.'

The men were huddled near the embers of a fire, steaming mugs in their hands. They glanced across as Miguel appeared, somewhat surly and ill at ease. Bear hefted his shoulders from the stalagmite against which he had been leaning and showed his broken teeth in a grin, delighted to see Angelita and making sure she was served coffee. Carlos lifted a hand in salute, his face glum, supporting himself on an improvised crutch.

'What's wrong with him?' Angelita asked Bear, sipping the strong, sweet brew.

'He fell and twisted his ankle, madam. It might even be broken.'

'I want you to see to it there's a strong guard in the tunnel,' Miguel snapped abrasively, Carlos's injury of little concern. 'Don't let anyone through. Shoot if you get any trouble.'

'Yes, *patrão*,' Bear mumbled.

'You can't do that!' Merran was shocked to the core.

'I can,' Miguel answered, and seized her upper arm in a vice-like grip. 'You still don't understand, do you? No one is going to stop me. If I have to kill every damned one of those who oppose me, then I will.'

'You'll never get away with it.' She tugged her arm free, yet was aware of a savage thrill racing along her nerves.

He was ruthless, amoral, powerful. Maybe, at another time, in another place, even another lifetime, she would have gladly thrown in her lot with him. But now? I'm no murderer, she thought.

He chuckled wickedly, in a great state of agitation and excitement. 'Who will know? Anything can happen out here. My men certainly won't talk. They wouldn't dare. And you, Merran, would you betray me?'

He held her to him and she could feel the hard rod of his erection pressing against her through his khaki trousers. He was aroused almost beyond control, adrenalin pouring through him, sex-drive mingled with the emotions of cruelty, violence and greed. The hands holding her shook, and she could smell the musky odour of his sweat.

'Well, would you?' he repeated, fingers like talons, bruising her flesh.

Fear was a strong aphrodisiac, and her vagina pulsed, nipples stiffening. 'I don't know,' she answered, daring herself to defy him, challenging him to take action.

'You won't.' His voice was low and persuasive. 'Not when you've seen the things I'm about to show you. Like me, you'll do anything to touch them, to own them, to dispose of them to the highest bidder. Isn't this what your grandfather intended?'

'He had no interest in making money from the venture. His satisfaction came from the thrill of discovery.'

'How very philanthropic! I'm not like that. Neither is Angelita, and neither are you, deep down.' He stared at her with those hypnotic eyes. 'I know you better than you know yourself, my dear.'

There was no answer to this and he did not want one, darting off into a passage leading from the gallery, and Merran followed, unable to resist this unpredictable man. Angelita had borrowed Bear's torch, and now twin beams played over tumbled boulders and treacherous crevasses as they advanced quickly, with Miguel leaping over obstacles.

'We're almost there,' he panted. 'No one else knows of its existence.'

Struggling to keep up with him, Merran's feet suddenly struck rough-hewn steps leading down into another cavern, smaller, more intimate, utterly bewitching. The trickle of water caressed her ear. Moisture shone on greyish, moss-spattered rocks. A waterfall sparkled, cascading from a fissure into a natural basin. A single cone of daylight radiated through a hole far above them. It had been deliberately constructed to land full-square on the stone representation of a man.

'Will you look at the size of *that*?' Angelita breathed, awestruck eyes riveted on his penis. Rearing up massively between his thighs, it was an impressive twelve inches long and capped with shining gold. Two slabs had been placed in front of him so that votaries could reach his sacred tool and worship with mouth or vagina or rectum.

'Aren't you glad you listened to me?' Miguel crowed, his flies undone, his own organ exposed, fingers stroking the swollen stalk. 'It's well hidden. I should never have found it if Carlos hadn't fallen down a shaft. I stumbled across it while we were trying to get him out.

Hardly aware of him, Merran paced round the statue, drinking in the noble domed forehead that bore a three-tiered crown, the slanting lids, wide nose and full lips. The eyes seemed to follow her, made of two glittering emeralds that reminded her of Nick's. The torso was naked, of staggering male beauty, the waist girded by a belt set with precious stones, the legs sturdy as tree-trunks, the arms banded by jewelled bracelets.

She was obsessed with the desire to touch the phallus, and lifted her hand, feeling the cold hardness of it, remembering the mind-blowing pleasure of Angelita's *godemiche*. How much more exciting to impale oneself on the mighty appendage of Priapus.

Was this what he was, a deity personifying male power?

The atmosphere of the cave was pregnant with force, as if charged by age-old rituals. Paintings illuminated the walls, the red and yellow pigments as bright as if executed yesterday. Gigantic men held their arms towards the sun, each blessed by a forward-pointing cock. Blood gushed from the throats of sacrificed animals. Bare-breasted women offered themselves to the god, their genitalia embracing his engorged organ, or those of his priests. Sheaves of wheat, vines and fruits, pollen-carrying bees, eggs and birds – every adjunct to fertility had been painstakingly copied.

'Earlier than we thought,' Miguel said, his breath catching in his throat as his fingers whipped up his climax.

'Thousands of years before, maybe,' Angelita chipped in. 'It's too artistic to be Inca or Mayan or even Toltec. Their work is clumsy and crude. Not like this.'

Merran was unable to resist the impulse driving her to sit on the floor, take off her boots and remove her trousers. Naked, she approached the statue and placed her bare feet on the smooth stones positioned before it. They had been worn down in the centre by generations of acolytes.

She dipped her fingers between her thighs. Her honey-pot was wet, luscious and warm, on fire with anticipation. She rested a hand on each of the god's shoulders, raised herself on tiptoe and slowly advanced her pubis, gazing into the bright jewels of his eyes.

The golden glans coaxed her portal apart, sending a chill rippling into her womb. Her vulva clenched, then relaxed as she pushed, gradually taking the phallus into her moisture-flooded depths. At first she felt uncomfortably full then, slowly and fearfully, she moved up and down on the alabaster-smooth surface.

'Can you get it all in?' Angelita asked, her face flushed, her hand inside her panties, clutching her mound. 'Hurry up, darling. I want to try.'

Behind them, Miguel gasped as his semen jetted out with such force that it spattered Merran's bare bottom. The warmth added to that gathering inside her. She arched her back and tried to bring pressure on her clitoris. Angelita reached round to help, her finger landing unerringly on that hot little spot.

'How many years, d'you suppose, since anyone mounted the god's prick?' she said as Miguel clasped her round the hips and she ground her rump against his semi-hard cock.

'Hundreds,' he said. 'Don't you feel privileged, Merran?'

But Merran was beyond thought, eyes closed, head back, her mind filled with images of past rites as she concentrated on the great stone thing chafing the lining of her love-passage, the tingling heat building as Angelita's finger rubbed the tip of her clitoris. She spasmed into orgasm, consumed by a deluge of such intense pleasure that she blacked out.

She came to herself to hear Angelita whispering, 'My turn,' and obediently slithered off her perch, hardly able to stand, her knees buckling. The comtesse tore off her trousers and took her place, crying out, 'You've made it so wet for me!'

'Was that wonderful?' Miguel asked, lodging himself at Merran's back, hauling her close.

'Oh, yes,' she rejoined as he slipped his hardening penis between the throbbing lips of her sex.

She knew what was coming but did not fight him, his fingers making circles round her clitoris, harvesting the juices at her vulva and spreading them up to the tight bud of her forbidden orifice. Then he forced open the puckered ring, and she screamed, the sensation dark, thrilling, a violent tightness that contained peculiar pleasure.

In her anguish she saw Angelita riding the stone cock, a frantic equestrian with a new kind of mount. Merran fell into the same rhythm, Miguel's thrusts accompanied by swifter movements on her love-bud. The pain was lessened, though the sensation was one of extreme tightness.

Angelita came with a yell, slumping over. Miguel increased his penetration of the narrowest, most secret part of Merran's body, his touch on her clitoris electrifying. She could feel red-black waves of pleasure crashing over her and cried out incoherently as he convulsed in his own completion.

He withdrew from her, and Merran felt a burning sensation at the mouth of her rectum, aching from his bitter-sweet violation. Angelita embraced her, caressing her face and hair. She smelled of female sweat and the oyster aroma of sex.

'I've something else for you to see,' Miguel said, smiling at them benevolently, a master pleased with his cherished pupils.

He took them to where the water splashed into a deep pool. Ripples disturbed the surface, but gold and gems flashed in the crystal clear depths.

Angelita plunged her arm in to the shoulder, trying in vain to scoop out the treasure. She straightened, her eyes bright, breasts rising and falling with excitement. 'Offerings from worshippers?'

'I think so.' Miguel sat on the edge of the basin, and spread himself over it to keep intruders away. 'Golden artifacts, jewels and trinkets. The kind of things women throw into wishing wells to bring them luck, or a baby, or a lover. We can easily remove them by diving or using nets. Think what the dealers will pay for such finds?'

'If there's any erotica, I want it,' Angelita reminded. 'I'd love a solid gold dildo.'

'You shall have it,' he promised, leaning over to kiss her lips.

'No one's having anything,' Nick shouted from the top of the steps. 'Get your hands up, Garcia. You too, comtesse.'

He stood there like an avenging angel, toting a gun instead of a flaming sword. The cave entrance was crowded with Indians, and Jon was in their lead, gaping at the statue. Seth, Liam and Terry backed Nick, armed and grim-faced, while Estefan paid special attention to Miguel, watching him like a hawk.

'I knew you were up to something,' Miguel bellowed. 'You're a crook, Slater. You were after this, too. I'll strike a deal with you. We share the treasure, fifty-fifty. What d'you say?'

Nick advanced steadily, keeping him covered. 'Sorry, Garcia. No deal.'

'You want it all?' Miguel was horrified.

'I don't want any of it. I'm working for the Brazilian Government.'

'A cop?'

'A private investigator. They'll be grateful you've found the relics for them. They might even overlook the fact that you came here without authorisation, intent on stealing a national heritage. Maybe they won't jail you after all.' Nick turned his frosty gaze on Angelita. 'As for you, comtesse – I guess your husband will buy your freedom, though I'd like to see you behind bars.'

Merran was on a plateau at the top of the escarpment. It had been discovered after they had mounted a set of worn steps corkscrewing up into the daylight from the Sacred Cave.

It was flat and verdant, covering a large area. Against the flaming western sky the jungle canopy far below looked black and leaping and alive, as birds swirled, seeking night-time roosts. To the north lay a long, dusky-blue mountain ridge.

'"Go and look behind the Ranges. Go!"' she quoted to herself, adding, 'Well, I looked, Brig, and I found treasure and I'm here.'

She lay on the short, mossy turf and linked her hands behind her head. Gazing up, she filled her senses with the peace of the tropical twilight, that moment when day and night change places. She could hear her companions laughing and talking as they gathered round the campfire a short distance away. A nightjar called wistfully from the bushes and the cicadas chirped. The mosquitoes had been left in the forest and her skin was healing.

Events had happened with remarkable speed. At one moment she was being sodomised by Miguel: in the next Nick was arresting him.

Adrian had filled in the gaps. Apparently they had followed at a discreet distance, had had a scuffle with the Garcia supporters, disarmed them and left them under guard, then gone on to reach the cave of the stone idol.

She was still confused as to Nick's part in all this and now she heard a footfall close by and he materialised. 'I've been wanting to talk to you,' he said without preamble.

'Right,' she replied, rolling over to lie on her stomach, talking with the side of her face resting on her folded arms. 'And I think you owe me some sort of explanation.'

He flung himself down beside her. 'It's simple. I was paid to do a job and I've done it. I work for anyone who'll hire me, and I don't come cheap.'

'The Brazilian authorities, in this case?'

'Right. We've been organising this operation for a year, ever since word leaked out about Garcia's intentions. They sent for me. I was in Bosnia at the time, but came over, discussed it with the powers-that-be, and got myself employed by him, sussing him out. We knew he was expecting you.'

'And the others?'

'Seth's kosher, he owns that boat, but he's a pal of mine and we've worked together before. Terry's an archaeologist and Estefan's a cartogapher. He's been mapping out the route. We'll hand this and your log over to the Ministry for Antiquities. They'll man a scientific expedition. Terry and Estefan will lead them to the cave. There, the relics will be examined, photographed, dated and catalogued.'

The idea of the god and his golden phallus being disturbed upset Merran. It amounted to blasphemy. 'The shaman must be present. He'll perform the correct rituals to ensure no one is cursed,' she insisted, adding, 'You should know such things are important. Didn't you tell me about voodoo and the Goddess Iemanjá?'

Nick smiled darkly. 'I did, the first time I shafted you.'

Merran quivered, tormented by memories of his ardent intrusion into the centre of her being. She tried to be cool, practical, saying, 'What will happen to them afterwards?'

'They may be brought back and displayed in Rio, or loaned to museums worldwide. Whatever happens, it can only help the national economy.'

'I'm glad,' she said sincerely, then shifted till she was half-sitting and sneaked him a sideways glance. 'How come you didn't put me under arrest, too?'

He looked at her with a humorous slanting of his green eyes. 'I may be nuts, but I like to believe you're innocent. I'll put in a word for you, Miss Faulkner. Any case, we've got a date. A hotel with the biggest bed they have, and satin sheets. This'll be pretty near impossible if you're doing time.'

'You've got a nerve.' She was moist with expectation, but not about to let him know it.

'Sure have, and ain't you glad of it.'

His hands were confident as they touched her, and she felt the stirring of her internal tides drawing her towards him. Moisture dampened her pubic curls and the bridge of cotton covering her vagina. She remained perfectly still as he ran a finger over the peak of her nipples pressed tightly against her T-shirt. But when he lowered his head and sucked at them through the material, her control snapped.

She moaned, rose above him and, kneeling, ripped off her top, breasts gleaming in the dusk, then removed her trousers and freed her legs. Nick lay prone beneath her while she undid his fly and opened it wide. His cock was already erect, jutting upwards like a rapacious cobra. She ran her fingers from its tip to the full orbs of his testicles.

Now she went down, taking him into her mouth, nipping and sucking. He sighed and strained against her lips, urging her lower, till his glans butted the back of her throat. His hands moved to her breasts, stroking, fondling, and she abandoned his cock momentarily, sliding back on his thighs so he might move his fingers in spirals on her clitoris.

She was confident and triumphant, entirely in charge, orchestrating this episode. Nick was hers to do with as she willed. Tough man though he was, she had the upper hand. She used her power without mercy, coming violently against his fingers, then resting her hands on his shoulders, lifting her body till her vulva hung above his cock. She eased her hips down, permitting him to press the triangle of his glans into her entrance – an inch, no more.

He gasped, feeling her heat, and she smiled into his

face, going lower, slowly drawing his prick inside her. She hunched over him, her tongue tasting the brown berries of his nipples. His hips arched as he struggled for the rhythm which would bring him to climax.

'No,' she said sternly. 'You must wait,' and she refused to let him move while she continued to torture the little nubs nestling in his chest hair.

'You're cruel,' he groaned, almost beyond control. His eyes were staring, beads of sweat running down his anguished face.

'You want to push it in and out?' she purred, continuing her torture. 'You really want to do that?'

'Yes! Yes!'

'Not yet.' Thank you, Miguel, she was thinking, feeling the pulse of Nick's desire buried deep within her. You've taught me well.

'Let me, witch,' he pleaded.

'All right, but no more than six strokes. I shall be counting.'

He obeyed her, controlling himself, and she counted each delicious thrust and retreat then stopped him. But it was getting more difficult for her to keep this up, ripples spreading through her from the joining of their bodies. Even while her fingers worked and pulled at his teats, so she was beginning to forget everything but the crying need to bring this love-play to its conclusion.

Breaking bounds, Nick thrust and bucked beneath her. His contractions filled her vagina as he grabbed at her hips, pulling her roughly down on his penis, hammering it home. The sharp sword of ecstasy splintered her resolve. And it was more than mere physical sensation; she felt for him, *with* him, as if he were part of her. It was scary, tremendous, pushing her to the brink of bliss, her heart and mind teetering on the edge of total surrender.

'What was all that about?' he mumbled an immeasurable time later, as she snuggled her face into the nape of his neck, sipping the sweat that pooled there.

'I don't know,' she confessed sleepily. 'Delirium, I think.'

'Fuck it, I feel like I've been pole-axed.' He sounded as bewildered as she.

It felt completely right to be in his arms, softly held in the aftermath. So right, in fact, that it terrified her. How could she possibly survive a day without having him with her, sharing her trials by day and her bed at night, his penis resting between her thighs?

I can't become dependent! It will destroy me, as it did my mother.

She released herself from him, reaching for her scattered clothing. He watched her, the light dying from his eyes, to be replaced by his customary hard green stare. 'Is that it?' he asked levelly.

'I don't know what you mean.' She refused to look at him, her head bent as she struggled to lace her boots.

'You know damn fine. When we get back to Manaus, to Rio, will it be goodbye?'

Merran swept up her hair with her hands, bunched it at her crown and secured it with an elastic band. She already felt prim and schoolmarmish, able to cope, her emotions tied, too. 'Probably. I don't suppose our paths will cross again. I'll be going home to take over Tawstock Grange, while you, no doubt, will be off on some James Bond mission in a faraway place.'

Taking his cue from her, he stood and zipped up, his shirt hanging loose and unbuttoned. 'I get the picture. Well, it was nice while it lasted, Miss Faulkner.'

With that he strolled away from her and did not look back. Merran watched him go, her heart like a stone within her. Then she shrugged and went to find Jon.

He had taken over a niche in the rocks, near where the stream flowed into the Sacred Cave. The light of a small fire glowed on him as he knelt there, drying out his long blond hair. His skin smelt fresh and tangy from his bathe in the ice-cold water.

His body bunched with muscle beneath that bistre skin, and all he wore was a little red *guayuco* containing his genitals. She touched his shoulder and his hand came up to cover hers. He turned, rose, and clasped her tightly to his big body, towering above her, truly a giant in stature.

'Merran,' he whispered, proud to have mastered her name.

'Jon.' She lipped his skin, loving the cool, smooth texture of it beneath her tongue. He stared down into her face with those blue, blue eyes. 'Listen to me,' she said, annunciating each syllable slowly. 'Tomorrow I'm leaving for the river. Estefan tells me you will escort us there, but no further. Why is this, Jon? I had hoped you might return to Manaus with me. I can trace your family, perhaps – take you to England – your real country.'

He scowled with concentration, trying to make sense of her words. She scratched pictures on the ground – canoes – the sea – but it was so hard to explain without language.

'You're confusing him, making him unhappy,' said

Estefan from the shadows. 'The shaman has told him all this, and Jon is torn. He wants to be with you, but can't leave the tribe, the only family he has ever known. Be kind, Merran. Let him remain in peace.'

Tears sprang into her eyes. 'Am I never to see him again? Will this really be the end?'

'It's best that way. Can you see him fitting into city life? He'd be miserable and frightened. Have this one last night with him, and keep it as a perfect memory.'

Jon was looking from one face to the other in puzzlement, and when Estefan had melted into the darkness, Merran lifted her mouth to his, finding the warm, eager welcome of his tongue.

A madness possessed her, born of the untamed night. She ran to the far side of the alcove, arching her spine against the uneven rock, breasts jutting, eyes bright with challenge. Jon growled and sprang after her. She leapt away, needing him desperately, but determined he should catch her first. She would play the game of rape with him, pretend to be a maiden from a warring tribe whom he was about to capture and ravish.

As she raced across the clearing under the white glare of moonlight, she dragged her T-shirt over her head and threw it. Striking Jon in the face, it blinded him for an instant, helping her gain ground. Dodging among boulders and through undergrowth, she glanced back to see him emerge from between two trees. Her heart pounded and a stitch clawed at her side. She stopped for a second, then set off again.

'Merran! Merran!' His voice echoed as he sped along behind her.

She was flagging, breath coming in great gasps, body slippery with sweat. His bare feet thudded, drawing nearer, and then she felt an agonising wrench as his hand plunged into her hair, dragging her up short. In a second they were rolling on the tussocky, fragrant grass.

Whimpering and thrashing, she was pinioned by his body, hot from the chase. Just for a moment she experienced the terror of a captive, a rush of panic and anger, coupled with a dark skein of excitement.

Biting, kicking, she twisted in his arms, beating at muscles that scarcely felt her blows. Jon grunted with deep-throated laughter and clamped his mouth on hers, forcing his tongue between her lips as she opened them to scream. One hand held her wrists and the other tore at her waistband. She writhed under him, freeing one fist and pummelling his back as the zip gave and he dragged her trousers down.

The fragile white fabric encasing her mound proved no obstacle to his lust, following the path of her pants, trapping her round the ankles. Trussed by her own garments, she was helpless to prevent him from thrusting into her wet vulva, his penis like tempered steel. Then she surrendered, freeing herself from restrictions. Her legs kicked up above his glistening back as he pillaged her vagina, and her arms clung round his neck.

Dimly, she recognised that this was how he used his wives, with no thought for their gratification. There would be none for her that way either, only savage pride in being mounted by the strongest male in the pack. Her loins responded to his savage jolts, and it was with the basic satisfaction of the primitive female that she felt him flood her with hot jets of semen.

By the time they reached the river Miguel's fever developed into full-blown malaria. It reduced him to a sweating, shivering, hallucinating wreck, robbed of any kind of fight. There was no longer a need for Nick and Seth to watch out for trouble. With their boss incapacitated, Bear, Carlos and the rest of the hellions decided to play it by Nick's rules.

'I'm so cold,' Miguel complained through chattering

teeth, lying under the canoe awning with blankets piled on him.

'The fever's burning you up,' Angelita soothed, on her knees beside him, bathing his yellow face with a cool sponge.

'Why do we bother to keep him alive?' Seth asked as he doled out a further dose of quinine. 'You're wasting your time with a bastard like that, comtesse. Look at the trouble he's got you into.'

'Trouble!' She glanced up at him, brows raised, violet eyes bright as Brazilian amethysts. 'I've never enjoyed myself so much in all my life.'

It had rained almost continuously since they left the mountains, but this journey riverwards had been much easier, due to the expertise of Jon and his warriors. No one went hungry. Snakes were clubbed and hornets' nests rendered harmless. The worst spots were avoided by using a different route, the swamps left behind and the canoes soon reached.

Now, they were reunited with those who had remained on guard over the boats, and sleeping-bags, hammocks and netting were stowed aboard the long craft, and fresh supplies handed over by the braves. Nick found a further cache of knick-knacks for them to take back to their wives, and they stood on the bank, faces solemn as they raised their spears in a farewell salute.

At Seth's signal, the oarsmen dug their paddles into the gurgling, fast-running water that would carry them swiftly downstream. Merran sat in the bow, watching through the veil of rain as Jon gave a final wave, then turned and was swallowed up in the jungle. The leaves shivered behind him and it was as if he had never existed, nothing more than a mirage conjured by her imagination.

'*Mon Dieu!* D'you realise what you've done, *chérie?*' Raoul bewailed, wringing his slender, perfectly manicured hands together. 'Now I shall have to service that silly old queen, General Valdez, in order to keep you out of prison. You really have been a very, very naughty girl.'

'Don't be cross,' Angelita pouted, supine on the massage couch in her suite at the Casa Valentine, while a splendid specimen of manhood wearing nothing but a towel about his hips eased every ache from her body.

Raoul sighed and came over to stand at the foot of the couch, admiring her golden-brown body. 'I can never be cross with you for long, as you know only too well.' He glanced at the masseur. 'Have you finished, Ramon?'

'I have, señor.'

'Very well. Angelita, my sweet, you're hairy as a stevedore. Darling creatures and I adore them, but I love to see your sweet pussy without a thick coating of fur. So ugly and unfeminine.'

She stretched her arms languidly. 'You may shave me. A husband's prerogative.'

She spread her thighs and he applied the razor, moving dextrously over her pubis, between her legs, and even as far as the rosebud of her anus. She flinched, sighed, hunger rising beneath the surface of her skin like an irritation.

No one knew how to indulge her appetites quite like her husband. He had a connoisseur's appreciation of her beauty, grooming and pampering her from the moment he had found her, a brash young prostitute in a wine bar. Her story of how she had been driven there by sheer wilfulness, not necessity, had amused and intrigued him, appealing to his decadent tastes.

She could smell the aroma of her own arousal wafting up as he lathered and scraped and washed the razor off in a small ceramic bowl. He patted her pubis dry with a fluffy hand-towel, and held up a mirror so that she might view it. Her whole cleft was deep pink and shiny, an exotic orchid with petals enfolding its heart, the stiffening pistil already near to pleasure's crisis.

Raoul unfastened the girdle of his burgundy silk robe, exposing the curling hair that matted his chest, thinning out to a line traversing his navel and blooming thickly on his lower belly. His soft, oily hands played over her nipples that peaked at his touch, and his lips took their place, nibbling at the eager teats. He leaned over her, and she took his shaft in her hand, the glans like the hood of a pinkish-brown mushroom.

He was a fastidious individual, his skin as highly perfumed as her own, a heady brew when combined with that of masculine musk. She relished the taste of his cock-head, her tongue darting round it as her fingers stretched back the foreskin. This roused her to the heights of libidinous fever as Raoul simultaneously fingered her wet avenue. He seemed transfixed by the sight of her clitoris swelling, deep red and ready to engulf her in orgasm.

He pinched the head between thumb and forefinger and she spent herself, gasping and convulsing as he rolled her on to her belly, spread her legs, anointed his prick with her copious juices and eased it past the anal ring and into the narrow recess of her rectum. Angelita braved the assault on her most secret place, pushing her hips hard against him. He moved in and out, his balls tapping the backs of her inner thighs, his excitement mounting till, very elegantly, he reached the quintessence of bliss.

He then withdrew, helped her rise, and wrapped her in a towelling robe. Proceeding to pamper her still further, he seated her on the divan in her boudoir, brushing through her hair with long sweeps of a silver-backed brush. As he worked at the tangles, they continued the conversation they had been having, as if nothing untoward had taken place meanwhile.

'And now poor Miguel is in a clinic recovering from malaria. I hope he's not arrested when he leaves,' Angelita remarked.

'No chance, *chérie*,' Raoul said, dropping a hand to check on her hairless pudendum. 'He knows far too much about the inclinations of top officials and has never been above resorting to blackmail. Don't worry about Miguel.'

'I do believe you've missed me, *caro*,' she murmured dreamily.

'Of course. I was a little worried, too. However, all's well that ends well. Tell me again about those gorgeous native boys, and I want to hear more concerning Estefan. He sounds absolutely delicious. Can't we invite him to dinner?'

'I'll see what can be arranged. Now I've something to show you.'

'A present? I love presents. What is it?'

She reached a hand under the divan and lifted out a long, foil-wrapped parcel. 'Here you are. I couldn't resist returning to the Sacred Cave unbeknown to anyone. I'd seen this glinting in the pool, caught on a ledge where I could reach it. Isn't it lovely, and won't we both enjoy using it?'

Raoul gave a yelp of delight as the paper fell open around a dildo of solid gold. This one was different, a double version with a perfectly sculpted penis at either end. Thus two lovers could insert it in their bodies simultaneously – twin pleasures, a double helping of delight. It was a sophisticated toy by any standards.

'*Dieu!*' he exclaimed in wonder, sliding his hands over this instrument of joy, a dozen glorious scenarios in mind. 'There's nothing new under the sun, is there, my darling?'

Chapter Ten

'You've survived, then? I'm so pleased to see you again,' Oliver Medway said, rising from his swivel steno-chair as Merran entered. He smiled, came across and took her hand, adding, 'How come I didn't get a picture post-card?'

'Sorry, Doctor. Guess I was too busy. You weren't alone. I forgot to send them to anyone. Most of the time it would have been impossible. There are no mailboxes in the jungle,' Merran replied, betraying her delight at seeing him again, body responding to his burly good looks as it always had and always would.

That familiar feeling tingled down her spine as she glanced at the white-surfaced couch where he had, many months before, examined her vagina and clitoris with professional skill, reverence and desire.

When dressing that morning, she had carefully selected red satin and lace open-crotched panties, a matching girdle with long suspenders clipped to thigh-high black stockings and a brassière with open tips. It had completed this wickedly expensive set of underwear, and she had openly admitted to herself that she had put it on for him.

She had paraded in front of her bedroom mirror, looking at herself as she teased her nipples through the embroidered holes and admired the way her golden-brown bush showed between the lace decorating the slit in her G-string. She had opened it further, fascinated to watch the pink line of inner lips protruding slightly between the outer ones, her clitoris just visible at the top. She had touched it with a fingertip, coaxed it from its cowl, then braced her legs on her stilt heels and masturbated till she came.

Standing in the consulting room now, she could feel the ambrosial juices from her vagina wetting the satin-covered cleft. She was sure she could smell her own perfume clinging to her fingers, even though she had washed her hands with scented soap. She had noticed before that the powerful odour was hard to remove, an almost indelible perfume, pungent as seaweed and ocean spray. Had she transferred it to Oliver when he took her hand in his? Would he, too, respond to its heady fragrance.

I've changed, she thought. Brazil has infected me with its dark sensuality rooted in basic passions, and my lessons with Miguel were a revelation. Or maybe it has something to do with this? And she reached up and caressed the little gold *figa* she always wore these days, remembering the giver and feeling constantly horny.

England had seemed smaller, colder, but infinitely lovely decked in all the subtle shades of autumn. She had been home for a month, allowing her body to adjust to the temperature, then making an appointment for a check-up after the rigours of exploring.

'You've lost weight and your hair's fairer,' Oliver remarked, regarding her closely. 'All brown and lean and tough. Was it hell?'

'Parts of it, but no, on the whole it was an experience not to be missed.' And as little vignettes flashed through her mind, so Merran felt nostalgia dragging at her vitals. 'You won't credit this, but I'm actually homesick for the place. A friend once told me that the jungle gets to you. It never lets go, calling you back, over and over.'

He gave a sceptical smile. 'The jungle? Or the men you met there?'

Merran could feel her cheeks flushing. 'There was no one in particular.'

You lying toad, she chided herself. What about Jon? He's haunted you, hasn't he? Wasn't it only last night that you reached orgasm in your sleep while you dreamed about screwing him?

And Nick – whom she had last seen leaving for the airport on his way to an assignment in Salvador. Nick, who had hardly spoken to her since he made love to her on the mountain top. Very official in their dealings, crisp, businesslike, getting her off the hook with the authorities.

'Did you manage to avoid malaria?' Oliver asked, bringing her back to the present.

'I did, but one of the party developed Falciparum.'

His face became grave. 'That's the most dangerous strain.'

'So I was told. He went into a private clinic in Rio, and is recovered now.' She recalled seeing Miguel when he came out, a sallow-skinned skeleton.

'No snake-bite?'

'No, but I was pestered by tiny flies. They're a horrible nuisance.'

'I'll take some blood samples,' he said, moving briskly to a wall-cabinet and returning with a syringe. 'Sometimes these things don't manifest till later.'

He's different, she thought, struggling to establish the contact they had had before she went away. But did she really need it? She had stopped seeking a father-figure. Miguel had put her right on that score. And the Amazonian rainforest had taught her salutary lessons about herself and her hang-ups.

Her mother's ghost had been laid to rest, it now seemed, the umbilical cord finally severed. Merran was no longer motivated by shades of the past, free to form her own conclusions and, maybe, to dare to become emotionally involved with a man in the not too distant future.

Oliver drew off a measure of blood, then looked down her throat and in her eyes and ears. He behaved so professionally considering the heat of their last encounter that she was amused, curious and a touch disappointed. It looked as if she had donned her new underwear for nothing.

The answer came as she was about to leave. Someone

tapped on the door and he called for them to enter. It opened to admit a tall, slender lady with dark hair and a warm smile, wearing a Hermès headscarf, a Barbour jacket and sensible brogues.

'Ah, darling,' he said, coming alive. 'Let me introduce you to one of my patients, Merran Faulkner of Tawstock Grange. She's just back from the Amazon. Merran, this is Audrey Parker, my fiancée.'

Merran wanted to tease him, to playfully accuse him of being a dark horse who couldn't remain faithful while she was away, but one look into Audrey's guileless eyes stopped her. Here was a person who obviously adored Oliver and would make him a wonderful wife.

'Congratulations,' she said sincerely. 'May I expect an invitation to the wedding?'

'Of course,' he replied and she read gratitude in his glance. 'And when may we hear similar news from you?'

When indeed, she thought, while she fobbed him off with a nimble excuse. She was approaching her mid-twenties. It was time to take stock and decide what she wanted to do with her life and who, if anyone, she intended to share it with. There was nothing to stop her resuming her drifting existence from one smart resort to the next, but this now seemed pointless.

Instead, she could begin to learn the management side of the estate, become the lady of the manor, the leader of the hunt, a respected figure in the area, called upon to judge entries at the agricultural show and maybe dabble in local politics. Somehow, it didn't appeal.

Adrian was waiting in the car outside the surgery. He had insisted on coming back to England with her, whereas Liam had gone to Kentucky with his American heiress. Lyn had returned, but they had waved goodbye to Angelita, Raoul and Miguel, who had decided to absent themselves on the Continent till the dust had settled.

Merran had been exonerated from blame, thanks to Nick, and had even received a letter of thanks from the curator of the Museu do Indio in Botafogo, who was eagerly awaiting further news of the find in the Sacred Cave. He had promised to send her a full report, and she had already been approached by a BBC2 television producer who wanted to film her story. News of such an important find had leaked out, and the papers had been full of it. Once again she had had to fend off reporters.

'Everything OK?' Adrian asked as she slipped into the driving seat.

'We'll have to await the results of a blood test. But I feel absolutely OK.'

'I'm glad about that,' he said, settling back and idly watching the passing view as they drove towards the manor. 'I was rather hoping you'd not come back to home sweet home with Jon's bun in the oven.'

She stabbed him an annoyed glare. 'D'you take me for a complete idiot?'

'Whoops! Sorry I spoke. I must say you're a tad tetchy. What's up, Doc?' He reached across and put his hand on her knee, letting it slide higher, thumb tracing over the suspender clip beneath her skirt.

'Nothing. Well, yes there is, I suppose. Life's so uneventful here. I enjoyed it at first, but now it's boring.'

'Ah, no gunmen, no natives – no danger. You get off on that, don't you?'

'Maybe I do.'

She was filled with the urgent heat of lust that Oliver had not satisfied. There had been too many fiery memories crowding in that morning and a dream fuck was all very well, but not as fulfilling as a waking one.

She left the road, swerved into a ride that penetrated the woods, and parked up in the leafy dimness. A hush spread over all. The peaceful hush of an English forest.

'No parrots,' Adrian said, a smile lifting his firm lips.

'No squawking macaws or howler-monkeys.' Her

eyes lingered on his mouth and the tip of her tongue came out. His was a nice mouth, humorous and kind and extremely kissable.

'You miss it. So do I,' he said, and slipped a hand into her jacket, tweaking her nipples into taut peaks beneath the silk blouse she wore.

The sensation was acute, forcing her to close her eyes and lean into him. She could feel him moving closer, his mouth touching her cheek, then her lips. 'I want you to fuck me,' she moaned as his tongue licked across them.

He unfastened the blouse buttons and gasped with surprised excitement as he saw her erect nipples poking through the tight slits. 'Wow!' he whispered, flicking and scratching at them. 'Bet you didn't buy this little number in Tawstock. It's the sort of thing a whore would wear. You have beautiful tits, Merran. I've always loved your breasts.'

She caught the underlying meaning of his words, saddened yet proud because this most eligible man loved *her* as well as her breasts. The sadness came because she knew she could not reciprocate. He was her friend, her tender lover, but her feelings towards him were almost sisterly. She could give him her body freely, but not that tiny, inner core which no one had ever touched: a particle of herself that remained inviolate.

She wriggled against his fingers and his fair, curly head lowered as he reached for her nipples with his lips, sucking at them strongly, becoming impatient and pushing the lacy cups down, freeing the full globes. Her womb clenched and her clitoris swelled. She could feel her wet pantie gusset pressing into the folds of her labia.

She stretched out her legs and opened them. Adrian reached for the hem of her skirt and began to ease it up over her stockinged thighs. He ran a finger round the tops, smoothed the tender skin on the inside, feeding on her mouth as he did so.

The front seat of a car brought back memories of teenage episodes when she had experimented with boys. She remembered the frustration; their fumbling hands and premature ejaculations when she had been left far from satisfied. There was no way she would have liked to be that age again. Now she knew her body, its needs and desires.

'Let's get in the back,' she suggested, pulling away from him.

That was better, more room to manoeuvre. And she rucked her skirt up round her waist and sat astride Adrian. His trousers were open and his prick hard. Her nimble fingers danced over its fiery red glans, then held the thick stem and guided it to her spread pussy-lips. She rubbed the head over them, pausing when the upward stroke reached her clitoris, subjecting it to special friction.

Adrian held her breasts in the palms of his hands, straining to lick and suck them. She watched his tongue busy at her teats, liquid heat oozing from her vulva. She coated her fingers in the dewy pool and moistened the tip of her love-bud.

As she played with it, so Adrian entered her, his cock penetrating deeply, and Merran screamed, arched her spine and flung back her head as a surging climax soared through her. He was inspired by her hunger, carried away by her lust, the frantic rotation of her hips, the pulsing of her vagina driving him to spill himself within her. She slumped across him, kissing his bare chest and the chestnut discs of his nipples.

'We go so well together,' he whispered, his breath tickling the velvety rim of her ear. 'Why don't we make it permanent?'

'Are you fortune-hunting, Mr Foster? Fie, and what will my lawyer say?' she teased, languid and content in the afterglow of sex.

'Your lawyer would be relieved to know you had a

husband to take care of you. He finds you a terrible responsibility,' he replied, hugging her close. 'What about it, Merran? The full works in Tawstock church – the wedding of the year, reported in *Hello!*'

Merran withdrew from him slowly, sitting up and combing her fingers through her tousled hair. 'It's a big decision. I have to be absolutely sure. Divorce doesn't feature in my future plans. It's so messy, especially if there are children involved.'

The fire went out of him, and his handsome face assumed an uncharacteristically moody expression. 'You don't love me,' he accused.

'I didn't say that,' she answered hurriedly, unwilling to hurt him. 'I don't believe I'll ever fall in love, not in the romantic sense. I'm too cynical.'

'You'd learn to love me,' he insisted as they straightened their clothes and returned to their seats in the front. 'We have so much in common – the same sort of upbringing and expectations. It would work, Merran, I'm sure of it.'

After lunch they changed into riding gear and took the horses for a canter through the golden glow of the autumn afternoon. The parkland dropped away and the wind whipped their faces when they reached open coun-try.

Merran reined in, looking down into the valley where the town nestled between rolling hills. She could see the grey rooftops of the older buildings, the brick-red of the new, and the Norman church with its tall spire and jumble of tilted tombstones. Her grandfather had been interred in the family vault there.

The ochre and chocolate fields resembled a giant's patchwork quilt. A snowy flock of sheep grazed, dotted like stars against the green. The silvery band of the river gleamed, and a postbox-red tractor accompanied by a daffodil-yellow muck spreader crawled slowly over the soil. Merran had the feeling that she had only to reach out a hand and pick them up, like children's toys.

This was her home, where she had been born in the local cottage hospital. It could not have been a greater contrast to the savage brilliance of Brazil, yet she loved both places with an intensity that made her heart ache.

'Time we were going back,' Adrian said, the perfect English gentleman in his tight riding breeches and hack-ing jacket. He glanced upwards, adding, 'That's a mackerel sky, and it means rain. I rather hate getting wet after the monsoons of the Amazon – developed a real aversion to it. I wonder if there'll be muffins for tea. I'll race you. Last one back buys the drinks in the pub tonight.'

'All right,' Merran said and turned her mare's head homewards, admitting to herself that what he had said earlier made sense. They were alike in so many ways.

On their return, they found a message on the answer-phone: Angelita's attractively accented voice saying, 'Merran, darling! We're in London, staying at the Dorchester. I just *had* to visit Mark's showroom. Haven't a thing to wear! We'll be with you tonight. Break out the champagne and invite some of your friends round for a party.'

'Who does she mean by "we"?' Merran said with a worried frown.

'Could be anyone from a pop group to a matador complete with his *cuadrilla*, and you know what they're like,' Adrian answered, laying aside his crop and hard hat and pouring himself a whisky soda from the massive carved sideboard in the oak-panelled drawing-room.

She did indeed – a collection of arrogant, swarthy gyp-sies who were a bull-fighter's assistants. She could hardly picture them mixing with her hunting, shooting, fishing and frightfully British neighbours. A hard-drinking, hard-screwing, coke-snorting rock singer and his band would be almost worse.

'I want to see her again, but dread the thought,' Merran sighed, and then pressed the intercom to summon Mrs Harvey and warn her there would be guests for dinner.

'This could be fun,' Adrian said, contemplating the fine malt brew in the cut glass decanter, then pouring another tot. 'Weren't you complaining that life was boring?'

'I take back all I said!'

But she had to admit to a quiver of anticipation as she dressed later. Even the sound of Angelita's voice had quickened her desires. That woman, with her sinuous body and exciting knowledge of sexual diversions – glamorous, worldly, offering untold pleasures of the senses.

The challenge of meeting her again had thrown Merran into a panic. What should she wear? It would have to be something devastatingly daring. 'Help me, Lyn,' she pleaded, standing naked in her walk-in wardrobe, rooting through the rows of gowns, racked by indecision.

'What a fuss! It's only your jungle comrade, after all. You've seen her looking a right mess, so what are you worrying about?' Lyn said in her usual practical way.

She was wearing a little PVC number she had recently purchased at the Fetish Market during the Blackwell Arts Festival. She was glad to be home where, during her free time, she could mingle with her mates, drink beer, listen to bands and behave in a way more conducive to her happiness.

Not that Lyn hadn't found the comtesse exciting: she had. But she was not awed by her or in any way lacking in confidence, recognising a wanton when she saw one. And, rich woman though the comtesse was, accustomed to hobnobbing with stars, in Lyn's opinion Angelita was basically a hot-arsed slut.

Merran settled for a turquoise-blue, ankle-skimming silk skirt cut low on the hips, worn with a silver charm belt and a white crop top. Both complemented her tan. She was bare-footed and bejewelled with silver bracelets, dangling silver earrings, and Nick's *figa*. She had become used to wearing little makeup, merely moisturising her face and adding a light dusting of powder. A touch of mascara, a smear of gold eye-shadow, lips a glossy coral and, hair flowing free, she was ready for anything.

On impulse, she had phoned Oliver and invited him and Audrey to dinner, kidding herself that they would have a previous engagement. They hadn't. He said they would be delighted to come. So be it, thought Merran, and handed the evening over to a power greater than herself. What would be, would be.

Oliver arrived promptly at seven-thirty, immaculate in an evening suit, with Audrey wearing a simple, impeccably cut navy chiffon two-piece and genuine but understated pearls. Merran was making small talk with them when Griffen stalked into the drawing-room and announced, 'The Comte and Comtesse Suffres have arrived, Miss Faulkner.'

She leapt to her feet. 'Are they alone?'

'No, miss. There is a Don Garcia with them and a Mr Mark Elvin.'

Miguel was there! Merran had not expected that. Her knees trembled as she remembered his possession of that most secret part of her anatomy.

'Show them in, Griffen,' she answered, maintaining her control. 'Then see their luggage is taken upstairs and inform Mrs Harvey. You'll have to lay more places at the dining table.'

'Yes, Miss Faulkner.' Griffen did not have to express

disapproval, he breathed it out through his pores. His very mien shouted, 'Foreigners!'

Angelita swept in. As usual, when she arrived anywhere her companions passed almost unnoticed. She sparkled. She scintillated. '*Cara!* My dear little Merran! And Lyn – *and* Adrian. My cup runneth over.'

They were embraced, kissed, enveloped in her all-pervading French perfume, while her slanting violet eyes fastened on Oliver and his lady. Playing to the gallery, she pirouetted, crying, 'D'you like my dress? Mark made it for me, didn't you, darling? Don't you think it's divine?'

The designer, wearing tartan trousers, a velvet jacket and frilled shirt, winked at Merran and said, 'She's over the top, as usual. I hope you don't mind my coming along?'

'I keep open house,' Merran replied, unable to keep her eyes from Angelita. Once the comtesse had resembled a soldier intent on guerrilla warfare. Now she was like a gorgeous showgirl, or a fallen angel.

Her honey-hued breasts, crowned with prominent nipples, were smooth and bare beneath a sleeveless, black-beaded top, her shapely arms were banded and looped with the same beads, her midriff naked, and she wore a diamond in her belly-button. Her slinky black semi-transparent skirt clung to her hips. It undulated as she moved, sometimes outlining the cleft at the apex of her thighs, sometimes not, a tantalising attention-getter.

Oliver was goggling at her, fascinated, while Audrey became excessively polite, as frosty as a winter dawn. Angelita saw this as a challenge and let loose the full blast of her seductive powers on the pair of them.

Mrs Harvey had surpassed herself and produced a wonderful dinner. A cordon bleu cook, she had lovingly prepared *hors d'oeuvres* of seafood, followed by pheasant in a wine sauce, game chips that melted on the tongue, home-grown baby carrots and mangetout swimming in savoury butter. There was a choice of desserts: a terrine of guavas, mangoes and passion fruit in a jelly of sparkling rosé wine; lemon soufflé, tart and sweet; mocha chocolate gateau awash with cream and sprinkled with chopped almonds.

'Better than the chow we had in camp, isn't it, Merran?' Angelita remarked, her tongue creeping out to lick over her red lips.

'Anything would be better than that,' Adrian exclaimed.

'Oh, I don't know. I got rather fond of fried piranha,'

Angelita went on, giving Oliver a teasing, sideways glance. 'Have you tried it, Doctor? There's a sort of revengeful satisfaction in eating it before it eats you.'

'I'd like to hear more of your remarkable adventures,' Oliver said, turning towards her in a way which any student of body language would have interpreted as sexual interest.

'So you shall, and your so-charming fiancée,' she promised, her eyes running over Audrey's long, slim legs to which the chiffon skirt adhered.

'My compliments to the cook,' Miguel remarked, seated next to Merran, as suave as ever, fully recovered from both malaria and his disappointment at losing the treasure. He, too, was considering the possibility of corrupting the cool Englishwoman who had promised herself to the doctor.

'Mrs Harvey will be pleased.' Merran had got over the shock of seeing him, now aware of other, less comfortable emotions. 'She's looked after the family for years. I couldn't manage without her.'

She cast her eyes round her guests, noting the interplay between them. How odd, she thought, to be entertaining these exotic strangers here, in sleepy old Tawstock.

She met Oliver's glance across the table and at the same moment felt Miguel's fingers invading her lap, pressing down between her closed legs to find the avenue between. He chatted amiably to Adrian as he did so, a wine-glass held in his other hand. Merran stiffened, struggling not to gasp at the warmth his touch invoked.

'Why, no,' she said with hardly a pause, continuing the conversation she had been having with Audrey. 'I must admit I've not met the secretary of the Women's Institute yet.'

'She's a very competent lady,' Audrey went on, dabbing her lips with her dinner napkin and then laying it beside her plate. 'And so much looking forward to having you residing at the manor. Your grandfather wasn't a lot of help, poor dear, though he was always generous with his cheques, but she feels a woman in charge here will make an enormous difference to her charity events.'

Merran was not sure whether she made the correct response, too aware of the heat seeping through her loins as Miguel's insistent hand continued its course. Nothing could stop him lifting her skirt, caressing her thigh and stroking across her pubic hair, softly and tantalisingly

She smiled and talked like an animated doll, knowing

he had her on trial. He was demanding that she come without anyone guessing what was happening. She was angry with him for putting her in this position, yet so excited that her lower lips were damp with love-juice.

Miguel smiled serenely as he pursued his quest, discovering that she wore no knickers. The tablecloth hid his activity from view. To those on the opposite side, it merely seemed that he sat in his chair and sipped his wine. In reality, his hand held Merran's naked mound and the middle finger frisked and played with her raw and sensitive bud.

Her nipples rose and her back prickled. The pleasure was almost unbearable, and she must contain it, keep it secret, let it spill over and swamp her and still be able to act the perfect hostess.

'I'd be interested to view the entire house, if you'll be so kind,' Raoul was saying to her. 'I'd very much like to compare the architecture with that of our château in the Loire Valley'

The hot ripples of impending orgasm were building in her as Miguel rubbed her clit relentlessly, yet with so much care that only his strong middle finger moved. Merran was in extreme distress, yet smiled and answered the comte.

'The house is Tudor, and it hasn't been altered much –

only modernised. My grandfather was keen to preserve it in its original state,' she murmured, sweat glistening on her brow.

Waves of pleasure built and receded – one, two, three – then higher – peaking into a light so acute and dazzling that she very nearly lost control, her body shaken by an orgasm that was painful in its intensity. Her face flamed, her hands shook, and Miguel said, smiling into her eyes, 'It's rather warm in here, isn't it, Merran? Would you like another glass of wine?'

He lifted his hand from beneath the table, resting it against his cheek then passing the fingers under his nostrils, inhaling her scent. Griffen leaned over her shoulder and refilled her glass.

Angelita was looking at her with a pensive, feline smile. Merran was sure she knew what Miguel had been doing and that it excited her. They probably all knew, had planned it in the car coming down. She could feel herself falling under their spell again, hungry for the sinful games at which they were so accomplished.

Oliver and Audrey did not linger long after dinner. He was on call, and shortly after they had settled in the drawing-room for coffee and brandy, his mobile phone called him away to a maternity case.

Merran wondered what would have happened had he and Audrey stayed. Was it possible that they would have been beguiled into taking part in one of Miguel and Angelita's little experiments in sexual deviation?

As it was, Miguel smiled round the dimly lit room and said regretfully, 'Such a pity they had to go, but never mind. There will no doubt be other opportunities to get to know them better. I think we might be more comfortable upstairs, don't you, Merran? I remember you telling me you had a most impressive bed.'

Go with the flow, she thought, languorous with recently achieved orgasm, good food and fine wine. Within a short time she was lying on the bed. It was like being enclosed in the heart of a flower, the foot and headboard writhing with carving, almost alive.

Miguel straightened up from tethering her wrists and ankles with silk scarves. 'You're right,' he mused. 'It is an impressive piece. I do so admire Art Nouveau. It's a most feminine form of design, expressing fertility, growth, life – plants straining out of the earth towards the light.'

The liquid notes of a Chopin nocturne drifted from concealed speakers, and from where Merran lay flat on her stomach, she glimpsed Raoul and Mark as they emerged from the bathroom, mother-naked and with arms interlinked.

Adrian and Angelita occupied the daybed by the window. His evening trousers were unfastened and his penis emerged, fully erect. The comtesse sat like a graven image, legs tucked under her, breasts cupped in her hands as she teased the nipples into dark red points of desire. Lyn was curled on cushions on the floor, her hand between her legs, the PVC skirt rolled up as she fondled the ridge of her clitoris.

'I think the good doctor and his lady might have been persuaded to join in the fun,' Miguel remarked, trailing a hand over Merran's bare shoulder-blades, waist and buttocks. His voice was thick with excitement, his thin face glistening with a light film of sweat.

Was he right? Merran had a feeling he probably was, adept as he was at reading people's innermost thoughts and desires. She was too tipsy to answer, allowing herself to drift, feeling as if she moved through an enchanted forest.

'You're still mine, aren't you, Merran?' Miguel hissed, and she was aware of something other than his hand at her back: the harsh caress of a leather tawse.

'Yes, Master,' she whispered, bracing herself for the blow that did not come – not yet.

'You didn't visit me in hospital. Why was that?'

'I couldn't, Master.'

'You were afraid to be seen associating with me? Is that it?' His voice was menacing. 'Nick Slater got you off. How did you pay him? Did you let him screw you, bitch? Did he penetrate your arse?'

'No – please, Master – don't punish me.' This was only a game, yet Merran was trembling with excitement, her loins lubricious, her clitoris chafing against the sheet beneath her.

The first flick of the tawse took her off guard. She screamed as the bundle of leather strips whacked across her bare bottom. At the same time, she could feel the burning heat linking with her centre, sending spasms through her.

She heard Angelita exclaiming and saw her bright eyes watching rapaciously while she sat on Adrian's lap, her back to him, her legs stretched wide over his thighs as she bounced up and down on his cock. Raoul and Mark were watching, too, from their place on the carpet, where Mark was on all fours while the comte shafted him.

The figures on the Gobelin tapestries hanging on the walls seemed to approve of the orgy taking place within Tawstock Grange – knights and ladies, troubadours and courtiers smiling slyly from their bowers, reliving their own pleasures of long ago.

Merran was alone. It was Lyn's week off. Her guests had departed and Adrian was in London on business. She suspected he had gone to buy her an engagement ring, though she had given him no direct answer to his proposal.

His attitude during her visitors' stay had been a liberal one, as in Brazil. There was not a jealous bone in his body, provided she did not fall in love with whomever she was shafting. He had resented Liam because he thought he might capture her affections.

Merran wandered through the house, letting it know she was now the mistress, and it welcomed and enfolded her as she communed with the ancestral portraits.

'Which one of them would you like as my partner?' she asked, roaming the Long Gallery with its massive bay windows at one end, the top leads consisting of heraldic crests in stained glass. 'Should it be Adrian, or possibly Miguel? He rather fancies himself as an English squire. Meanwhile, you'll have to content yourself with a petticoat government.'

She found she liked her solitary state, taking a tray to bed and reading far into the night, making little forays into the town, swimming in the indoor pool, bringing herself to orgasm if and when she felt like it.

But returning from the public lending library one lunchtime, she found a message on her fax machine. It read, 'Arriving Heathrow at 18.00 hours. Virgin. Flying from Kennedy. Nick.'

Her spirits soared and her heart thumped. She was immediately plunged into agitation. Ignore it, part of her said, that cold, cynical part that refused to yield. If you don't turn up, he won't bother you again.

Go on. Take a chance, urged the other side, the romantic, optimistic, tentatively hopeful side.

She rushed upstairs, passed an indecisive half hour choosing an outfit, then settled for trousers and a sweater, swung her bag over her shoulder and headed for the garage in the stable mews.

It was raining, a fine drizzle that looked set to last. The windscreen wipers were hypnotic as she took the motorway, heading for the airport. She put on a CD and Puccini's *Tosca* swept her away, as it always did. What did anything else matter when she could listen to the sublime sounds of the maestro's music drama telling its violent story of sadism, passion and religion?

What am I doing here? she thought at one point. I

could be perfectly happy as a spinster. I don't need any other man's voice in my ear except Placido Domingo's. Why am I travelling miles in the rain to meet an uncouth roustabout like Nick? I must be mad.

She found a parking space. Got thoroughly wet in the process. Waited in the enormous entrance area. She consulted the noticeboards. They flicked and changed. There was an announcement. The plane was late. It should be landing in fifteen minutes.

She guessed what was happening up there. The jet would be circling Heathrow, awaiting an approach time from air-traffic control. Merran went off and got a cup of coffee.

Fool, she lectured herself. Hanging around waiting for a man. Why don't you go home? She drank another cup, then had to find the Ladies and consequently rushed to the reception hall, afraid that she might have missed him.

'Oh, come on!' she whispered, whipped into a fever of impatience. 'Let me just see him, then maybe I'll go right off him.'

He appeared, running down the staircase, taller than she remembered, cleaner, positively wholesome in a lightweight draped linen suit.

His green eyes fixed on her, reducing her to a jelly. 'Hi

there,' he said in that deep, drawling voice that connected directly with her G-spot. He dumped his bag on the ground and swept her into his arms, kissing her with supreme thoroughness and confidence.

She wanted to fall to the marble flooring with him, open his trousers and connect with his penis. They'd get arrested, but what the hell?

He was hardening against her belly, and his breathing was shallow as he growled, 'Let's get out of here.'

'How did you know where to find me?' she gasped, her arms holding him so tightly that her breasts were squashed flat against his chest.

'It's my job to find out about people.' He seemed as confused as her by the emotions gripping them.

'Why? I thought you'd given up on me.' This is ridiculous, she thought dizzily.

'No way. I never give up.'

They left the airport, found the car, slung his bag in the back and sat there in silence, smoking, suddenly awkward. Then he leaned forward and pressed the CD button. Music swelled, filled the interior, filled the difficult silence, building a bridge between them.

'Ah, *Tosca*,' he said. 'And that's the recording from Rome, if I'm not mistaken.'

Merran gulped. 'You like classical music?'

'Mad about it. I'm not a complete Philistine. Education at Harvard, I'll have you know.'

'I didn't know. In fact, I don't know the first thing about you – your parents, your background, nothing,' she said, more bewildered than ever.

He grinned at her in that quirky way which turned her upside down. 'Too true, lady, but I'm going to tell you. There's plenty of time. I've not taken on anything else for the while. No, I said, there's a certain lady in England who needs someone like me to take care of her. How about me becoming your minder, Miss Faulkner?'

Merran smiled as she switched on the engine. 'I'll consider it, Mr Slater. I'm on my own at the moment. My housekeeper and butler are taking a vacation, but I'm never afraid there. Have the latest in security systems.'

'And you're wearing the *figa* I gave you. That keeps you safe.'

'How did you know?' Her voice went up an indignant octave. 'Well, really!'

He grinned disarmingly. 'I had a hunch. May I see?' And he leaned over and slid a finger into her cleavage, finding the amulet, but lingering there.

She almost hit another car, swerving just in time.

'Sorry,' he said unrepentantly, his hand remaining in the warmth of her breasts. 'Am I putting you off?'

'No,' she lied. 'I've never been more together.'

'Liar,' he whispered against her lobe, nipping at her earring and setting it swinging. 'Miss Faulkner, I came here to fulfil a promise.'

'And what was that?' I shall have to pull in at a layby, she vowed, or there will be a serious accident. I just can't concentrate with him so close to me. Surely, oh esteemed and noble ancestors, this can't be the man you want for me?

'I said I'd spend a week with you in a hotel, and we'd be in bed the whole time, between satin sheets.' The purr in his voice was beyond resisting.

'No hotel. I'm driving you to Tawstock Grange,' she said, trying to ignore the hand which had stopped tormenting her breasts and come to rest in the hollow where her thighs joined her body. Impossible, when the blood was racing through her veins and her loins yearned for him.

'Oh, well, I guess that'll do,' he drawled, so easy and natural that she wanted nothing but to reach home with all speed, rush him up the grand staircase, tearing off his clothes en route, and fall with him into the depths of her fantastic, fairytale bed. Then he added, 'D'you have satin sheets?'

'No, Nick,' she said breathlessly, taking a quick glance at his face. It was serious now, the lips pressed together, his eyes glittering with passion. 'Satin's too slippery and I want to be able to grab hold of you. As it happens, my bed is spread with fine sheets, but they are made of silk – wild silk.'